FAITH and LOVE

FAITH and LOVE

Stories by

Grace Livingston Hill

and her mother

Marcia Livingston

Compiled by

Jenny Berlin

Anglocentria
Aurora, Colorado

This is a work of fiction. Names, characters, places and incidents are products of the authors' imaginations or are used fictitiously. Any resemblance to actual persons, living or dead, or to events or locales, is entirely coincidental.

A Note from the Publisher . . .
Faith and Love is a collection of stories that originally appeared in magazines and newspapers published between the years 1893 and 1904. This anthology has been produced with every effort to retain the flavor of the original stories with only minor changes to update spelling and punctuation. You'll find this book reflects many of the feelings and attitudes prevalent at the time of the stories' original publications. The stories may contain references that reflect mores and opinions that directly conflict with today's prevailing sentiments.

FAITH AND LOVE.
Copyright © 2015 by Anglocentria, Inc.
P.O. Box 460458
Aurora, CO 80046-0458

E-Book ISBN: 978-1-940896-64-9
Print Book ISBN: 978-1-940896-65-6

CONTENTS

Introduction

Grace Livingston Hill is one of the world's most beloved writers of Christian fiction. I discovered her books when I was in high school; my friend Starlinda (isn't that a great name?) gave me her copy of *Job's Niece* to read. I loved the book and soon began collecting copies of Grace's books for my own little library.

Grace was a wonderful story-teller—a talent she came by naturally. Her mother, Marcia Macdonald Livingston was a writer, as well. Marcia wrote books and short stories under the name Mrs. C. M. Livingston. Her serialized stories often appeared in *The Interior* magazine; and she co-wrote Christian novels with her sister Isabella Alden, who was the best-selling Christian fiction author of her time.

Grace grew up in a home filled with creativity, a love of reading, and a strong work ethic. She learned the letters of the alphabet by clicking on the keys of her Aunt Isabella's typewriter. She learned the art of writing a short story from her mother Marcia.

At an early age Grace discovered she could earn a

living by her writing, just as her mother and aunt did. Her first book, *A Chautauqua Idyl* was published in 1887; and with that publication, Grace joined her mother and her Aunt Isabella in creating inspiring, uplifting and memorable Christian fiction for women.

Marcia encouraged her daughter and often edited her manuscripts before Grace sent them off to her publisher.

Grace wrote over one-hundred novels—all of which remain popular today. Less popular are her short stories—not because they are any less well-written, but because they are more difficult to find. Her short stories appeared in magazines and newspapers in the early years of the 1900s and copies of those publications are rare finds today.

The same is true for stories written by Marcia Livingston. They were published in the 1890s in magazines that went out of business long ago, their records scattered or destroyed; only a few issues can be found in libraries and museum collections. Their scarcity makes them all the more precious.

In this volume, I've compiled a selection of short stories by Grace Livingston Hill and Marcia Livingston from the years 1893 to 1904. When you read them, you might see similarities in the ladies' writing styles. You may also notice how uplifting their stories are, and how each story comes with a thoughtful lesson. Most of all, you may notice that a key element of each story is the message of God's love for us and the peace and joy we may know through Jesus Christ. Both women lived lives of abiding faith in God and sought to share their Christian beliefs through their writings.

For me, this collection of short stories by Marcia Livingston and Grace Livingston Hill now occupies a treasured place in my library, right beside the authors' full-length novels, so I can read them again and again.

I hope you, too, enjoy this collection of stories by two remarkable writers of Christian fiction.

—Jenny Berlin

Jenny Berlin is the author of Ask Me Again, *a Christian romance, and she is a regular contributor to the IsabellaAlden.com website and blog.*

FAITH AND LOVE

GAIL HATHAWAY'S OFFERING

by

Grace Livingston Hill

(Originally published in 1901)

GAIL HATHAWAY'S OFFERING

Gail Hathaway knelt before her open trunk in the girls'
dormitory of the Glenside Preparatory School with a
smile of anticipation on her face. She had been tying up
tissue paper parcels with a dainty baby ribbon. There
was a lace scarf for mother, gold studs for father, a copy
of Ernest Seton-Thompson's latest book for her brother
Richard, ten-pins and a lovely doll for the little brother
and sister at home, with a woolly lamb for the baby. Gail
had been saving her pocket money for months to make
these presents all that her heart desired. She pictured,
for the hundredth time, the delight of her dear ones on
Christmas morning.

There were other packages, too, for old friends and
servants, and a small box from the jeweler's, which she
patted tenderly as she tucked it in a safe corner where it
could not rattle about. This contained a handsome ring
for Doris Deane, her dearest friend, who was going home
with her to spend the Christmas holidays.

Gail paused in her packing to muse on the happy
times they would have. Dick was going to take home his

best friend also, John Howard, a senior. Gail was just a little afraid of him, for he seemed older and wiser than the other boys in school, and she felt, when with him, as if he could see straight through her, and knew all the silly things she had ever done. He was a fine scholar and athlete, broad-shouldered and handsome. All the girls were anxious to stand well with him. Gail was in a flutter of anticipation over having him at their home for a whole week. She and Doris had planned out every minute of the time, and meant to make the most of their vacation.

Into the midst of her meditations came Doris's knock. Hastily pulling down the trunk lid, she went to unlock the door.

"What is it, Doris? You look as if you had seen a vision," she asked.

"I have," said Doris gravely, "and it's out at the hall window now."

Gail opened the door and looked out, then walked swiftly to the end window, where stood another girl. There was nothing to be seen but roofs, and a distant view of the railway station. The girl by the window is not looking out, and there were traces of tears on her face.

"Has it stopped snowing?" asked Gail in an indifferent tone, to which she received no reply. Then she went back to her room.

"Doris, what in the world do you mean? There's not a thing out there but that tiresome Estelle Barclay, with her freckled nose against the window pane."

"Abigail Hathaway," said Doris, with very red cheeks, "you and I have got to do something that we won't like one bit."

"Now, Doris Deane, what has your dreadful conscience got up? You needn't go to proposing that I ask that hateful little thing out there in the hall to go along with us, for mother said I could only bring one on account of Aunt Anna being there. Anyway, I wouldn't do it. She is the most spiteful, disagreeable, stupid girl in the school."

"Gail, dear, listen. *I'm* not going home with you! Don't look that way! I cried all night about it, and I know it spoils all your plans, but I can't help it."

Both girls clasped each other, and wept at the mere thought of the disappointment till Gail sat up, and said energetically:

"Now, Doris Deane, what's the use of crying? This is nonsense! You *shall* go. Tell me all about it, and I'll soon straighten you out, and show you you have grown morbid."

Doris sat up, pushed back her hair from her flushed face, and tried to smile.

"Yesterday," she she said, marking out the pattern on the bedspread with her forefinger, "I got a letter from auntie —"

"The mean thing!" exclaimed impulsive Gail. "She didn't take back permission after she said you might go!"

"No," said Doris, "but she said she was half-sick, and that if I decided not to go with you she would not feel sorry to have me home to help with the rag carpet."

"And you would go home and meekly sew rags all the vacation, instead of having good times as we have planned? Doris Deane, I'm ashamed of you! If she was real sick and needed you it would be different—but a *rag carpet!*" And Gail's vehement words failed to express the contempt she felt.

"Listen," said Doris, gently, a spasm of pain passing over her face as the picture of her disappointed hopes was placed before her. "You know you and I have promised to follow Jesus—to do just as he would like to have us do; and I can't help feeling he wants this. It wasn't the rag carpet nor auntie's words. I know she is lonely, and I don't think she belongs to Jesus. I've been a good deal troubled that when I lived with her I never tried to show her, by my life, what Christ was to me. I think I must've been disagreeable and hard to manage sometimes when she went against the grain."

"Doris! *You* disagreeable? Impossible!" said Gail,

leaning over, and kissing her.

"I'm coming to your part now, Gail," said Doris, gently. "My part is to give up all the fun, and go home and make a carpet, and see if I can make auntie love me a little — or is love Jesus, anyway. But I'm afraid you won't like your part, and maybe," she paused and looked up at her friend with wistful eyes, half-afraid to finish, "maybe you won't do it."

"Thank you, Miss Deane, I know I'm not as good as you; but if you are bound to be a martyr, I'll follow you to the stake. Tell it, quick!"

"Well, then, last night after I got in bed I heard a queer little choking voice in the hall. You know my room is quite near that window where Estelle is standing. The transom was open, and I listened and heard it again, and presently there came a real sob, followed by a catchy breath, with an 'Oh, dear!' in the quiveriest voice you ever heard. It went on for a long time. Every little while there would be a sort of moan, and then it would be smothered. Once I heard: 'Nobody loves me—nobody on this whole Earth loves me—and they never will.' And then the sobs came close together. I felt all frozen up, as if I had heard burglars, but I couldn't go to sleep, and I couldn't help hearing.

"'All the girls are going off to real homes to have good times, and nobody wants me,' the voice said. 'I've just got to stay in this old-school school with that horrid Miss Maddock, and have no nice times at all. Oh, mother, *mother*, why didn't I die, too, when you did?' After that there was such loud sobbing I was sure one of the teachers would hear, but nobody did. I got up softly, and managed to unfasten my door without making any noise, and there stood Estelle Barclay in her nightgown. I knew her outline against the white window the moonlight outside. She had slipped out there to cry all by herself. You know she has a roommate. I think she heard the noise of my door, careful as I was, for she suddenly glided back to her room like a ghost, and I didn't hear any more of her; but I could not get to sleep the rest of the night."

The tears were dropping from Gail's cheeks.

"We'll take her home with us, of course, Doris, dear; mother will arrange it somehow, and not mind what we tell her all about it, but you must go, too. I couldn't do it alone. And I know well enough you just dragged in your aunt first as an excuse to get me to take Estelle. There is no real need of you're going home, now is there?"

A bright blush suffused Doris's cheek, but she answered quickly: "I must not go with you, Gail, dear. Indeed, it would not do. You know that if I did Estelle would just be number five all the time. We would forget her and carry out our plans, and she would feel that she was 'de trop' at once. That would not be giving her the happy time I meant at all. I want you to have her all to yourself, and be lovely to her as you are to me; make her your friend, and do every sweet little service for her and give her your confidences, so far as you can, just as you do me. Indeed, I believe it will do more for Estelle than anything else in the world can do. She is starved for a little love. If I went along you would be nice and polite to her, and make her perfectly comfortable, you know, but she could not help feeling that you and I were dearer to each other than she was to anyone."

"Well, aren't we, Doris? And, besides, love doesn't come at a bidding. I couldn't, I just *couldn't* take Estelle into the same place, and what's more I *wouldn't!*"

"That's just it, Gail, you wouldn't. You just ask Jesus to give you the *will* to do it for his sake, and you can. I'm not afraid of my dear Abigail. But of one thing I am certain; I am not going along to stand in the way."

They talked long, these two girls, and the trunk stood waiting to be packed, while argument and entreaty and tears and gentle pleading vied with each other to turn to tender consciences. But Doris was firm. Indeed, her friend saw that every word only made her more decided for the sacrifice. At last Gail rose and went to wash her swollen face. Every few minutes a fresh supply of tears would swell into her eyes at some fresh remembrance of disappointment.

"What will the boys say?" said Gail in sudden dismay.

The pink stole into Doris's cheeks.

"Your brother is a gentleman. Dick will be nice if we ask him to, and it doesn't matter about John Howard."

"Dick will be nice if *you* ask him, you mean. But I think it does matter if John Howard thinks I make special friends of girls like Estelle Barclay."

But it was all over at last. The invitation was given and accepted with as much Christian grace on the one hand and surprise on the other is could have been expected. The neglected trunk was hustled together in a hurry, the white box pressed into Doris's hand at the last moment, the good-byes said, and the party of four started on their journey.

Doris had told Gail when she came up to help her lock her trunk and find her gloves that the boys had been told of the change of plans and were just splendid about it, but Gail expected to find reproach in their eyes nevertheless.

Estelle Barclay was seated beside her, unmitigatedly happy, and talking very loud. Every sentence she punctuated with a burst of giggles. Gail found it difficult to remember that only a few hours before she had been touched to tears with pity for this girl. She blushed over the attention Estelle attracted and blamed herself for the "scornful" look, as Doris called it, that she knew she wore. Doris and she had knelt hand in hand but a few minutes before beside Gail's bed, and prayed silently for strength to be of service to Estelle. Gail tried to forget her annoyance and remember her promise to Doris. She gave herself up to being agreeable to her companion, and a little later when the seat in front of them was vacated, and the young men came from the back of the car to join them, she was surprised to discover that she was actually growing interested in Estelle's sorrowful, empty life.

A surprise was in store for her. Dick Hathaway, with a smile as pleasant as he would have given Doris, raised his hat to Estelle and said:

"Miss Barclay, suppose you sit over here with me and let John and Gail talk a while; you two ladies must be weary of each other by this time."

Estelle, nothing loth, arose with a burst of giggles, and Gail could not hide her annoyance at the loud voice with which she responded. Her face grew crimson with mortification when, looking up, she met the kindly sympathy of John Howard's gray eyes—and was there a light of admiration in them as well?

"I have been hearing for an hour of the virtues of Miss Deane," he said, as he sat down; "but, upon my word, I think there is another person who goes ahead of her in brave self-sacrifice, and that is the young woman who has actually taken into her heart's innermost sanctuary, for a time, a most congenial spirit. I think your part is a great deal harder than Miss Deane's, and, if I may be permitted to say so, I think you are doing it beautifully. I can't help thinking of a Bible verse our minister at home often quotes: 'Offer him the sacrifice of gladness.' I think you are doing it. That it is a sacrifice is obvious to all who know Miss Barclay; but you have cheerfully given her your gladness, and you have made her happier, I suspect, then she has been in many years. It's about the best gift a human being can offer Christ on his birthday. If I can be of any help I shall be glad, for I belong to him, too."

Gail's eyes filled with tears of pleasure as she thanked him. She began to realize that the sacrifice was not half so great now, for she had dreaded the disapproval of this young man more than she had known.

As for Dick, he was thoughtfulness itself throughout the journey, and, indeed, the entire vacation. Gail suspected Doris's hand in that.

It was really beautiful to see Estelle's pleasure in the dear home. All the fun they had planned was carried out. Of course they missed Doris, and is still was often a trial; but one day she had a long talk with Mrs.

Hathaway, and after that she seemed to grow more gentle.

Two days before the return to school Estelle came down dressed for a journey, and announced that she's going back to school to help Miss Maddock correct the papers. They had all been so lovely to her that she wanted to pass it on to someone else, and she whispered to Gail, as she was leaving: "I'm going to try to be a Christian, like you, you dear!"

Gail's heart gave a great throb of joy as she realized that it was more blessed to give than to receive.

Dick seemed to have a great many errands to the station and telegraph office that day. He made some excuse for not going skating with Gail and John in the afternoon, as he had to drive to the village for the mail, and, for once, he omitted to ask them to accompany him. But when they returned, there was Doris sitting by the fire, with Dick radiant beside her, and mother Hathaway smiling over their surprise.

"I think it was the first real Christmas gift I ever gave to Christ, Doris," whispered Gail, after they had talked it all over, as she kissed her good night, "and I thank you for helping me to put away my selfishness and give it."

FAITH AND LOVE

SAINT JULIA

by

Marcia Livingston

(Originally published in 1894)

SAINT JULIA

Part 1

The first intimation that she was to have a daughter-in-law came to Mrs. Dale one morning when she was "tidying up" her son's room. It fell from under his pillow when she shook out the bedclothes; a letter addressed to "Mr. Stephen Dale" in a feminine hand. The mother eyed it curiously then slipped it from the envelope and unfolded it—a dainty sheet with a faint odor of violets.

She sat down on the foot of the bed and put on her spectacles. The very first word nearly took her breath away. "Dearest"! Indeed! Who could be writing to her son in that style? She glanced at the signature. "Julia" no other name. Now who in the world was Julia?

If, as Mrs. Dale read on, a faint suggestion crossed her mind that she might be transcending the mother's privileges, she dismissed it summarily. Stephen had always shown her his letters—why should she not read this? If he had any he wished to hide, then she ought to see them and make sure that he was not going wrong in any way, forgetting for the moment that her son was not a boy in his teens.

However she may have fixed it up with her conscience, Mrs. Dale read the letter through. Then she sat a long time, her head bowed on her hand, the silence occasionally broken by a long drawn sigh. Stephen had a secret from her! In all the thirty years of his life this had not happened before to her knowledge. But this was not the bitterest drop in the cup. He loved somebody better than he loved her! She who had devoted her life to him, especially the last ten years, when they were "all in all" to each other, being quite alone. The woman who was thought by those who knew her best to be a prosaic common-sense woman belied that reputation now as she buried her face in her hands and sobbed long, dry sobs.

Stephen was engaged! That was plain. The thing she had feared years ago and then ceased to fear as time went on and he remained indifferent to all womankind except herself, had come. Stephen was going to marry! And what then? She could not give up the old place where most of her life was spent and go away, neither could she live there alone. Step aside, be a mere nobody in her own house and let Stephen's wife rule, she would not. And two mistresses of one establishment were out of the question. Oh, there was no end to the trouble and perplexity of it all.

She picked up the letter and looked it over again. The most prejudiced eyes have to confess that the handwriting was neat and legible, and the spelling correct. It so happened that Mrs. Dale was a prime speller herself and had only contempt for a poor one. She had an eye, too, to the diction and knew that it was above the common, and while there could be no doubt that Stephen Dale was held in high regard by the writer, there was yet a delicacy and reserve apparent which placed it above criticism. As she restored the fateful letter to its hiding place there was a half-formed wish in the mother's mind that there had been something amiss with it.

Mrs. Dale had risen earlier than usual that morning because she had certain Christmas preparations to make, two or three old friends having already been invited to dinner. She had gone up to her son's room with a brisk step and cheery spirit, looking forward with zest to a day of busy cares. She came back to her kitchen with dull eyes and flagging step. Life had changed its current since she left that room. The pleasant past, all those years of quiet companionship with her son, were virtually over. Henceforth she should not be first in his heart. That other one, "Julia," would have the place.

While she stoned the raisins her mind went on a search amongst all the girls in town and out, of whom she had ever heard. Which of them was named Julia? She could not tell. While she chopped the citron and mincemeat the clatter of the knife against the bowl seem to say, "Julia! Julia! Julia!" It was a sort of a mean little name, she told herself, yet remembering guiltily at the same time that it was a Scripture name. She distinctively recalled having read a chapter in Romans last Sunday and noticing the name—that Julia was a saint and Paul had sent a kind word to her. But that was neither here nor there. It didn't prove that all Julias were saints by any means.

Stephen Dale was somewhat to blame for his mother's having settled it in her mind that life was to go on with them perpetually as it had done the last ten years. In their confidential talks he had often said half jocosely that for his part he could not imagine how one ever came to a final decision in the choice of a wife; and then in a more serious mood would declare that marriage was a lottery, that some of his friends were so mis-mated that it had been the ruin of them, that he was very sure he should never marry until—"until I must," he said.

"Until you must?" his mother asked, knitting her brows in perplexity. "What do you mean?"

"I mean," he had answered, with a light, half-tender, half merry-twinkling in his brown eyes, "that if any being so dear and precious that I could not do without her should ever cross my path, why, then the 'must' would come in. But don't look so solemn, mother dear, as if you were about to surrender me. The one I have in mind will never stray down so far as this earth. If she should, she will not cast so much as a glance at me."

So the years had gone on, Mrs. Dale, meantime, settling to the conviction that her son would always be happy in his home with no companionship but her own. And the tie between them was peculiar. Stephen was the kindest and most thoughtful of sons, and the mother—she had an idol and his name was "Stephen."

Julia Fletcher, the ideal being who had at last materialized in Stephen Dale's world, lived in a neighboring city. Their meeting was a chance one, as we are apt to speak of that which is in reality the fulfillment of Divine plans—in which Mr. Saybrook, banker, had not the least idea he was furthering when he introduced Stephen Dale to his young sister-in-law, who happened to be spending the evening with them. The two had not been aware of each other's existence before, though Mr. Dale had for several years visited the city at stated times and transacted business at the Saybrook bank. The banker had always felt a warm liking for the young man and yielding to a friendly impulse, invited him home to dinner.

It was the old story of that strange mutual attraction. Stephen Dale was surprised to find that his journey home that night was beguiled of its usual tediousness as he told himself exultingly:

"She has come. I have found her, the one I will win if I can."

And Julia Fletcher's cheek took a brighter glow as she realized that every word and look of this chance stranger had been treasured up by her and dwelt upon with pleasure; a discovery followed by severe self-condemnation.

Stephen Dale made any amount of trouble for himself because he did not manage well at this crisis of his life. If he had but confided in his mother from the first, and bespoken her sympathy in the time when his heart was distracted with doubts and fears as to the success of his suit, all might been different. But he shrank from confessing to his practical mother that after all these years of stoicism he had surrendered his heart quite suddenly. Moreover, he had begun to feel of late from certain words of hers that she would be averse to his marriage. He grieved that it should be so, for the aim of his life thus far had been the promotion of her happiness. So deferring from day to day to acquaint her with it, the engagement was an assured thing before Mrs. Dale had heard a lisp of it. It happened to be the evening of the day in which she had discovered the secret for herself that Stephen told her at last. They sat together a few minutes in the twilight as he poured of the story of this great joy that had come to him, and rehearsed the perfections of the lovely girl he had won. The light was too dim for him to see the expression on his mother's face or she would not have been favored with certain little confidential details, which once he had begun, fairly told themselves. When he ended by asking:

"Can't you bid me God-speed, mother?"

There was only silence. Mrs. Dale, through the whole of that troublous day, had not for a moment entertained the thought of trying to dissuade her son from marrying. When matters had reached the point that Stephen allowed any girl to call him "dearest," it was a hopeless situation. He would be true as steel, despite any obstacles. She might as well make the best of it. So she came to the martyr-like resolution to bear her sufferings in silence. Her son should never know what this step of his had cost her. But alas for human nature and its results. When she heard Stephen's voice speaking in low impassioned tones of her who had won his heart, the spirit of jealousy—dormant and unsuspected all these years—roused itself and took possession. She could not speak the word she had honestly intended should be kind. And so the silence.

Stephen cast a keen look at her through the uncertain light, then realized that his avowal had been extremely sudden, went over to her, laid his hand upon her head and gently smoothed her hair according to an old childish fashion of his. Was it a stifled sob he heard? His mother who never yielded to tears!

"Mother, dear," he said, "don't try to speak about it now. Some other time."

Then he went away to his own room, sadly disappointed, it must be confessed. And this was but the beginning of many disappointments. As the days went on his mother grew silent and reserved toward him and did not encourage him to speak much of his approaching marriage. And she allowed a slight indisposition to serve as an excuse for her absence when the wedding day came. Stephen felt deeply aggrieved at this and down in his heart believed that if it had been the annual meeting of the Woman's Foreign Missionary Society she would have got there somehow.

The wedding and the bridal trip were over and Mrs. Stephen Dale found herself in the parlor of her new home waiting to meet her mother-in-law. They had arrived by an earlier train than was expected and Stephen had gone in search of her.

And now as she looked about her, the first cloud that

had overshadowed the bride appeared on her horizon. She had not looked for magnificence in her new home. Stephen had assured her it was quite plain. But this room! It was simply unbearable. The carpet was immense figures—staring bouquets of very bright red and blue and yellow roses. The square center table without a cover. The slippery horse hair furniture, and the bloomed wallpaper! It was beyond belief that so refined a man as Stephen should have come from this home. What a background that paper would make for her lovely etchings! But then another survey revealed to her that there was no room for her pictures. The walls were already adorned with likenesses of ancestors, with the tomb of Washington set in vivid green and with hair flowers and wax flowers and all the other clutter of a past age.

"If now the belongings of this room were very ancient," reflected the bride, "paper hangings with a shepherdess design, say; carpet soft tinted by age, and furniture of quaint shapes; scrolls, claw feet and brass trimmings—why, that would be charming." But now, with all these gaudy colors, at a time when furnishings and delicate tints of greens and grays prevailed, well, it was common to the extreme.

"How could Stephen?" But there she pulled herself up. Thoughts disloyal to Stephen should not be entertained. Probably, manlike, he had given no attention to these matters, or his tastes had been overruled. She could doubtless effect a change in time, at all events it should not spoil things for her now. This was one of her crosses, this parlor, it might be.

It is but due to Stephen to say that a short time before his marriage he had put in a protest concerning this very matter. He did not know just what was in fault, but felt in a perplexed way that there was an indefinable something in Julia's home that was lacking in theirs. Hitherto he had not given the least attention to anything of the sort; now he proposed that they re-furnish the parlor at least. His mother opened her eyes in astonishment.

"What for?" Had he money to throw away? The carpet was body Brussels and would last years yet, and the furniture was good as it ever was. If it had been good enough for them it was good enough for "her." What would he do with that if he bought new? For her part she was not willing to put an extra cent on it.

Stephen groaned inwardly. His mother was an old-fashioned woman and if he were to try to make her understand about the changes in refined taste, the requirements of which he did not comprehend in detail himself, it would be a hopeless undertaking. The house and the furniture belong to them both and she had her rights in the matter. It is true he was now able to set up an establishment of his own, but that would not comport with his ideas of filial duty, as his mother was alone in the world but for him. So he comforted himself with the thought that he and Julia would bring it all right sometime, somehow. However, he did go to the east room upstairs and look it over, wondering what he could do to make it look more as if it belonged to Julia. It was clean, but stiff and unwelcome-like, with not a touch of prettiness anywhere, even his man's eyes saw that. The ingrained carpet had a large geometrical figure and the cane seat chairs stood about primly. He despaired. He would wait and let Julia fix it up herself sometime. He wanted though, to put some little thing there to show that he thought about her, so he bought a delicate little white and gold rocker and placed it in a sunny window, and on the window seat a pot of violets, feeling with intense satisfaction as he surveyed it, that one spot in that house was redeemed and fit for her—the Queen.

Mrs. Dale was surprised not to meet a dashing black-eyed beauty in her daughter-in-law. This slim girl clad in gray blue to match her eyes—earnest eyes—with straight brows, sunny waving hair and a mouth whose curves were both firm and sweet seemed not so formidable a creature as her imagination had conjured up. And the young wife—dreading to meet her mother-in-law, lest she might be after the style of the parlor, blousy and loud—breathed a sigh of relief to find a woman of intelligence and dignity of manner, who spoke quietly, and seemed not abashed in the presence of the city bride, even though her neat grey gown was after a fashion of long ago. On the whole Julia was favorably impressed and decided that it would not be hard to learn to love her. She could've wished the greeting had been more motherly and wondered a little to herself that it was not. Stephen had not told her of his mother's opposition, for really he felt it scarcely amounted to that, and she had expressed more by her changed manner than in any other way. He felt assured that Julia would soon win her and all would be well.

Part 2

Unwisely enough, there had been no previous understanding as to the management of domestic affairs now that a new member was added to the family. Stephen, inexperienced, thought, if he thought at all about it, that matters would arrange themselves. It is not to be supposed that his mother had not meditated long and anxiously upon the subject and quietly settled it. She had no idea of abdicating at present; and as two heads of one institution were out of the question, there was nothing to be done if Stephen brought home a wife but for her to take her place as a daughter in the family and share its burdens, herself, Mrs. Dale senior, the head, of course. In the church she had for years managed the missionary society and the sewing society, and everything else that needed a general. It would be strange indeed not to manage her own household.

Into this home, without in the least understanding the state of affairs, came the son's wife, loving, bright and energetic; in the first flush of her new joy, brave to meet and overcome all that might not be to her liking. She did not look forward to a life of idleness. Probably her duties would be much as they had been at home, assisting in the care of the house, directing the servants, etc. She was not averse to this, but on the contrary, rather eager to prove that her education in these matters had not been neglected.

The first few days after her arrival she moved about as in a dream trying to realize the change in her life. Then she leisurely unpacked her trunks in the big bare east room, stoutly resisting the inclination to drop a tear as she recalled the pretty nest of her room from which she had flown. As if anything mattered, when Stephen was here!

She wrote letters, and read, and strolled about the pleasant country lawn and finally, just as Mrs. Dale had come to the private conclusion that Stephen's wife was "a good-for-nothing creature," awoke to the fact that her mother-in-law was without a servant, doing all with her own two hands and that this was her usual custom! Julia was dismayed. Was she, too, expected to give herself up to cooking and washing dishes? She had not counted upon that. She hastened to offer her assistance in the meantime, half-shyly proposed that a servant be secured and each of them superintend her in turn, adding, "Mother and I did that the last two years and it worked admirably."

Now, Mrs. Dale was an old-fashioned housekeeper and a veritable Martha. The idea of a slatternly girl desecrating her spotless tables and floors and nicking her ancient china was not to be thought of. She rejected it utterly, even though Stephen urged and insisted.

"Be patient a little while dear," he told his wife. "With additional labor, mother will soon see the necessity of help, I am sure."

He did well to counsel patience for the young wife needed it. It seemed that she could do nothing to please her exacting mother-in-law. There was a certain fixed law regarding manner, time and place for the veriest trifles. She was not trusted to perform the smallest service without surveillance and direction, and was often in a peremptory way bidden to drop the work in hand and take up something else, possibly some distasteful task to which she was not the least accustomed. So there was no end to the ways in which each annoyed the other.

Julia was one morning preparing to sweep the parlor when Mother Dale intercepted her as she was going in, broom in hand, and exclaimed:

"Oh, don't take that broom! I only use it occasionally there. I take a whisk broom and dust pan. It saves the carpet, makes it last as long again. Have you never learned that yet?"

Julia was surprised and amused, but she kept it to herself and bringing the required implements, bent meekly over her work, feeling as she brushed the dust into her eyes that if it were in her power she would like to demolish the hideous carpet. While she rapidly dusted the furniture she tried to relieve the stiffness of that uncomfortable room by placing the sofa across the corner and dragging some chairs into more easy positions. Entering the room shortly afterwards she found them restored to their former places. In various ways she was made to feel that her vocation was simply to obey orders.

She set the table for dinner adorning it with a vase of nasturtiums and a lovely centerpiece, that and the vase among her wedding gifts. Her own mother would have exclaimed in delight over the effect, but Mother Dale, regarding them with contempt, exclaimed, "What nonsense!"

One morning the son's wife decided that a clean tablecloth and napkins were necessary. No sooner had she made the table fair and orderly than the mother-in-law emerged from the pantry and eyeing it with a frown demanded:

"What does this mean—clean tablecloth and napkins

this morning?"

"Why, we always change ours in the middle of the week. I thought you did, too."

"We do not. We can make our washings big enough without it."

This was trying to the dignity of the young wife— that she had not even so small a right as this in a home that was called hers. A flush came to her cheek and irritated words to her lips; but she did not speak them. It was Stephen's mother.

After several weeks had passed with constant, though mostly silent, jarrings between the two housekeepers, Julia gradually ceased to take any care upon herself but worked under orders, hoping thus to escape some fault findings—and this was more to the mother-in-law's mind. She came to the kitchen one day when dinner was in course of preparation asking:

"What can I do to help?"

"You may pare those potatoes," Mother Dale answered.

Julia looked aghast at a pan of the ugly tubers standing on the table. Seldom in her life had she performed that, to her, particularly distasteful job. She cast a glance at her pretty blue cashmere gown and white muslin apron. She had expected to set the table and perhaps concoct some dainty for dessert. But this—

this ugly work! Could she? Would she? There were her hands, too, plump and white, with rosy fingertips. The sturdy business would stain them. Then Stephen would wonder how they came to be grimy. It was odious that she should be asked to do it. This was work for a servant. A turn of the shapely hand sent out a flash of light from her wedding ring just then. Ah, that ring! It stood for much to her. Trouble with Stephen's mother meant worry and sorrow for him. It was settled. The lace cuffs were turned back and the hands made a swift dash at the potatoes before resolution had time to fail.

Mother Dale had seen the hesitation but she shut her lips tighter and went on making pies. She almost indulged in a grim smile, too, at the desperate plunge of the white hands into the pan; and counted it a victory.

"Why shouldn't Stephen's wife pare potatoes once in a while as well as herself? To be sure, she was working in a dreadfully awkward way and the pairings were twice as thick as they ought to be, but so she was doing it at all, that was enough for the present."

As soon as the obnoxious potatoes were finished Julia fled to her room and the irritations of many days which had now reached a climax found vent in tears. She was like many another saint of us—sometimes forgot her high calling and allow the old nature to get the upper hand.

It was not, she told herself, that she was unwilling to do menial tasks occasionally; but this only opened the way for more drudgery. The whole thing was a sort of tyranny—refusing to employ a servant—which of course necessitated her doing work she did not wish to do. She was more like a servant herself than a wife and daughter in this house. It was hard, too, when she had done her best that Stephen's mother should dislike her. Why was it? It was all humiliating. She would not have her own family know it for the world. Oh, if they had but a home of their own, however small and plain. She had half a mind to tell Stephen she had reached the end and they must go away. But of what was she thinking? Had she not promised herself repeatedly never to complain to her husband of his friends? She picked up a little book that lay opened by her side where she had often found the word to set her straight, and read:

"Nothing else but seeing God in everything will make us loving and patient with those who annoy and trouble us. They will be to us then only the instruments for accomplishing his tender and wise purposes toward us. If our Father permits a trial to come, it must be because it is the best and sweetest thing that could happen to us and we must accept it with thanks from his dear hand, that is, we must like God's will in the trial."

It was the right word for her. "And I have been

murmuring against God's will for me!" she said to herself. "I will not anymore." She was a true saint after all, this Julia.

Her husband would soon be at home, mounting the stairs two at a time, inquiring for her. She hastened to remove traces of tears, and all griminess from fingertips, and while she did it, softly sang:

"Thou sweet beloved will of God,
  My anchor ground, my fortress hill.
My spirit's silent fair abode,
  In thee I hide me and am still.

Upon God's will I lay me down,
  As child upon its mother's breast;
No silken couch nor softest bed
  Could ever give me such sweet rest."

Thus far Stephen had only surmised that his wife had trials to bear of which she did not speak, for to his great surprise and sorrow his mother seemed to have taken on irritability entirely foreign to her nature heretofore. What did it mean? He was utterly perplexed. But neither Stephen nor his wife ever guessed at the true cause of much of the trouble.

The mother had been for years accustomed to her son's constant companionship after business hours. But now when he came home he sought not her but his wife.

They sat and talked by the hour, volumes, or they went off together to ride or to walk, leaving a mother devoured with jealousy, hungering for a word or look. They forgot her, they left her out. Who shall say they were not somewhat to be blamed as a pair of thoughtless children? And she magnified and misunderstood every trifle and made no allowances. After a time she let them severely alone, would not even go to church with them, poked along by herself ahead or behind with a grim face; thinking bitterly within herself, "how different it was with me once, I had my boy's arm to lean on of a dark evening. It's all over now. I shall be a lonesome old woman the rest of my days."

And the two absorbed in each other went on oblivious. It is true Stephen often said, "Come on, mother; aren't you going with us?" just as if he didn't care a straw whether she did or not. Her heart swelled with bitterness day by day toward the interloper who had caused her so much unhappiness. It never occurred to her that she herself was the chief cause. She had grown suspicious, too; imagined that Stephen's wife made complaints and that when they talked in low tones it was about her, when in fact it was but the little fond things that married lovers exchange and which would lose half their preciousness if spoken in the hearing of others. Her heart would fairly rage within her at the thought that Stephen had allowed anybody to come between them and speak against his mother to him. Many sleepless nights were spent by this deluded mother, tossing about, brooding over her troubles and shedding hot tears.

It did not mend matters that Julia, despite her struggles to the contrary, felt the effect of her mother-in-law's brusque words and ways. Her joyous nature was repressed. The name "mother," which she had briefly taken up the first day, froze on her tongue, and the many winning words she wished to speak turned into silence.

Once started in this way, each continually misinterpreted the other. The younger woman had not the remotest idea that the elder was in reality afflicted with almost a monomania, that at her best she was conscientious and affectionate, and that every morning she knelt, asking for grace to bear the trials of that day, chief trial being her daughter-in-law. The dear girl didn't know she was a trial to anybody, encompassed as she had been by love all her life.

A trial came to Julia though when they were at breakfast one morning. The next-door neighbors' little girl knocked at the side door with a message from her mother to the effect that their cook's sister, an efficient German girl, was about to change her situation and they could secure her if they wished.

"Now," exclaimed Stephen with great satisfaction as soon as the door had closed on the messenger, "let's have her at once. You know the Putnam's consider their girl first class; probably her sister is just as good."

Julia, too, put in an eager word that in her home they had always found the Germans to be excellent help. But a frown was gathering on the mother's face.

"What are you talking about?" she asked an rasped tone. "I haven't said I wanted any help. I have worked all my life so far and expect to the rest of it."

"But mother, you should be taking care of yourself a little more now," Stephen urged. "You are working too hard. You will break down."

"Well, then, I'll be out of the way and you can have things to suit yourselves."

"Mother!" Her son exclaimed, sorrow and gentle reproof in his eyes. For an instant there was a softened look on his mother's face, but it vanished at Stephen's next plea.

"I do wish you would consent to take the girl. I want Julia to have more time to go out with me."

That was the last straw for Mrs. Dale. "If you two are managing this house you can make your own plans, but if I am, I will do it," she said with emphasis.

"Let us manage it for a time, do mother, and you take

some rest," he pleaded.

"Humph!" in a scornful tone, was the only reply vouchsafed.

Stephen Dale had not dishonored his mother by undutiful words since he had reached manhood. He was sorely tempted now to say something sharp, but he kept silent and soon left the room and the house, and as he parted with his wife at the gate, said sorrowfully:

"Oh, dearest, I don't know how all this is to end. It was utterly unlooked for by me. Truly, I would hardly know mother in the new character she has taken on. Perhaps you feel that we ought to go and live by ourselves, but how can I desert my mother when she is growing old?"

"No, dear," his wife answered, her irritation vanishing before his distress. "Of course we cannot go away; your place is here. Don't fear for me," and she smiled briefly up into his face.

"Oh, you treasure! And you will be patient and try to love her a little despite it all, for my sake, and for Christ's sake?"

She bowed her head with sweet solemnity. And yet in the solitude of her own room, with Steven gone, that other self within each soul suggested to her that it was sorely vexatious to be so trammeled and baffled, to have scarcely no time for music or reading and bits of writing she had begun to do for periodicals. If she had but definite duties to which she could give certain hours, it would be more tolerable; but that was out of the question.

There was much drudgery through those autumn days, when the air was full of odors of canning, preserving, jellying, jamming and picking, sweet and sour. The young wife grew very weary of it all, of the gloomy house and her gloomy mother-in-law. She was lonely in that chilly atmosphere and longed inexpressibly for the love and brightness of her old home, and her own dear mother, not but that all these feelings vanished at the first sound of Stephen's step. Sometimes, too, it must be confessed she forgot to rejoice in the will of God and was on the point of giving up in despair and allowing the angry retorts that troubled on her lips to take shape in words, especially when the mother was unusually exasperating, insisting on a thing being done just so and so after some ancient fashion when the young housekeeper believed she was following the most approved rules. It was not at all easy to give up her own way sweetly. She might have yielded to the tempter possibly and spoken bitter things, but for the remembrance of her husband's words, "For Christ's sake." At such times she set herself the task of preparing the unlovely potatoes and would even wipe up the oilcloth about the sitting room stove, a big old-fashioned square of it and no small job—Satan should see that he could not conquer her on that line. If she was not growing in favor with her mother-in-law, she was growing in grace, as these dreary days went by.

Stephen saw it and reverenced her yet more. Once his mother, vexed at some household matter, complained of his wife when she was out of the room. With a white face and in a tone that awed her, he said, as he got up and walked the floor excitedly:

"Don't, mother, don't! You may find all manner of fault with me, but do not, I beg you, ever speak another word against my wife. I cannot—I *will not* bear it."

"You allow her to talk against me, though."

"Never! Never! She would not for the world. She is one of the loveliest beings that ever lived on this earth. How anyone could take such an insane prejudice against her I cannot imagine."

And then he went out, not trusting himself to further words, went to brood over his perplexing state of things, growing each day more unbearable. And what remedy was there? His mother went to her room, and if the son could have seen her his heartache would have been still deeper, as she sat on the edge of her bed, her shoulders bent—with hard work for him, her idol—her grey head bowed in her hands, the hot tears trickling through her fingers, thinking within herself:

"My boy has turned against me. He can see no good in anybody but her. I wish I was gone out of his sight forever."

Part 3

At this crisis there came a visitor into the household—
Stephen's aunt, a widowed sister of his mother, who
lived in Chicago with her daughter. Aunt Lucretia
Parker, or Aunt Crete as she was familiarly called by
nieces and nephews, was one of those bright, strong
women who act like a tonic upon certain other people.
Gifted with an unusual amount of shrewdness and
common sense, she had always been a sort of oracle in
the family, and a favorite, despite her tendency to rule
and a tongue inclined to be satirical. She was in the
habit of expressing her mind quite freely to her
relatives, administering advice or rebukes as she saw fit,
and they were accustomed to swallow them like
medicine, sometimes with a wry face albeit. Stephen
was glad of her visit just now, for his mother had always
been greatly influenced by her. Who could tell what
might come from one of her clear-cut talks?

Aunt Crete's eyes and ears were remarkably keen.

She had not been in this house long before she knew many things that had not been told her. For one thing, her favorite nephew carried a burden and had lost his light-hearted ways. The reason was not hard to find; his mother was not fond of his wife. Moreover she had grown irritable and tyrannical, while the young wife carried herself with sweet dignity in the midst of the most trying circumstances. The observant eyes of the new aunt saw this color sometimes deepen in her cheeks when her mother-in-law was especially exasperating, and noted that instead of sharp retorts, there was silence or a soft answer. And there was a sort of forbearing patience about the way she performed menial tasks to which she evidently was unaccustomed, that aroused the pity and admiration of the one who studied her.

In one of her talks with Steven Aunt Crete asked with characteristic directness:

"Why don't you keep a servant, Stephen? There is lots of work in this house."

His troubled look as he answered, "I have tried most earnestly to bring it about. You musk asked mother about that, Aunt Crete," told the story.

"Yes, I know," the questioner told herself. "That's one of Maria's stubborn posts she has stuck down. What in the world does she mean?" And hereupon she resolved to read her sister a lecture at the first opportunity and try to smooth the way for "that child." As a first step she proposed that Stephen should take his wife for a few days' visit at her father's.

"Get her rested up a bit," she told him furtively, "while I take care of your mother."

This plan needed no urging upon the two who were to carry it out. They had been gone a few days when one afternoon the sisters settled themselves for an hour's chat over their sewing. Each had it on her mind to speak upon a rather delicate matter to the other, when a good chance should come.

Aunt Crete had long rested as a burden on her sister's mind because, though not exactly an unbeliever, she had never definitely declared herself as a Christian. Mrs. Dale had resolved during this visit to try once more to arouse her sister's conscience. So with her head bent low over the tablecloth she was darning, she asked:

"Lucretia, don't you think it is time you were a church member?"

"What for?" asked Aunt Crete, counting the stitches in the heel of a stubbed little stocking she was knitting for the Children's Hospital.

"What for? How you talk! You know what for as well as I do. You didn't learn the catechism through when you were a little girl and get chapter on chapter in the

Bible by heart for nothing. You ain't a heathen."

Aunt Crete answered carelessly, "Well, when I see it makes a difference in your life—being a church member—perhaps I'll consider it. You have been one these forty years, you know, and you haven't seemed to make much headway. I can't see as your religion helps you or anybody else."

Mrs. Dale was accustomed to blunt speech from Lucretia and would bear much from her without taking offense. She winced at this, though, and said in an injured tone:

"Of course I don't profess to be perfect, but I try to do right in the main. I keep the Commandments, and I attend church and prayer-meeting always, and give to the poor, and to all the objects of the Board, besides doing more than my share in the sewing society and weekly meetings."

"What lack I yet, eh? I remember it told in one of those chapters I learned long ago about some folks who paid tithes of mint, anise and cumin, and omitted the weightier matters."

"Well, speak out now," Mrs. Dale said, with heightened color. "You've got something on your mind; you always did say just what you pleased to all of us and we swallowed it."

Aunt Crete laughed. "Oh, you'd be like all the rest of

them if I did—you would get mad and there 'twould end. You church members pretend you want to overcome your faults, and if anybody so much as hints you have any, off you go like a match. Do you really want me to tell you what seems wrong with you?"

"Yes, go on."

"And you won't be mad?"

"Maybe not."

"Well, I guess I ought to. I don't know much about religion, but I have a sort of hankering to set things straight when I see them awry. And I don't know how to do it in a nice, smooth way. I have to come right at it roughshod, Maria," and Aunt Crete laid down her knitting and fastened her keen, not unkindly grey eyes upon her sister. "If I were as good a woman as you are, I'd want to go the whole length and be better still."

"What do you mean?"

"I mean I should want to make my home a happier place than this one is just now, and I'd try to get that deep scowl off my forehead and speak pleasantly as you use to. I know just what's the matter. Your letter when they were married helped me to guess. You had an idol in Stephen for thirty years. You didn't want to give them up to anybody, and you're bound and determined not to see any good in his wife. That spirit is of the devil, I don't care who has it. Now Stephen is married. It's done!

You don't want him to separate from his wife, do you? Why can't you take her in and count her your daughter, and hide her faults, if she has any—bear with them just as you do Steve's faults, and let her have a little to say how things shall go? Why, she has no more rights than the cat. They haven't said a word to me, but one would be stone blind not to see they are not happy as things go. Stephen's wife is a jewel, I think, to bear it patiently. Just put yourself in her place. Suppose when you married instead of setting up an independent household, you had gone to your husband's home and lived there just like a child under age, at beck and call of your mother Dale, with incessant fault-finding besides! Would you have stood it long? Stephen looks fairly desperate when things don't go right. Mercy on me! Why don't you have a good time and make everybody else? Stephen's wife would love you to death if you'd let her. And it must be pretty doleful for her with him gone all day and you cross-grained, and she used to a different sort of life, coming from a beautiful home Stephen tells me!"

"I'm sure she has a good home here," Mrs. Dale interrupted grimly.

"Well, you ought to go out into the world a little and see how other folks live. Why, Maria, excuse me, but that parlor is enough to set one's teeth on edge. Can't you trade off that bloomed carpet for something quieter and get rid of those horsehair chairs that make me feel as if I was sliding down the cellar door when I try to sit on them? Take out all that trumpery that must've come out of the ark—wax flowers and hair flowers and leatherwork. Take them all up to your own room and let the young folks have something fresh. You and Stephen have the money enough. Nobody has such outlandish things around nowadays. It just shows what good stuff there is in that girl that she doesn't rebel outright. I declare, if I were you and couldn't make up my mind to have it all different, I would tell them to go by themselves. Not a soul of you as having a good time now."

Just here occurred a diversion. Mrs. Blake, an old friend of the sisters who lived a few miles away, came in upon them quite unexpectedly to spend the night and see Lucretia.

It was fortunate, too, for Mrs. Dale had arrived at the stage where patience ceases to be a virtue. Her temper was up and she was only waiting for a pause that she might treat Lucretia to a "piece of her mind." She welcomed the guest, however, and made some delicious biscuits for tea, and showed her all proper attention but managed to get along without bestowing a look or a word upon her sister.

She excused herself early on plea of a headache. Her head always did ache when she was angry and she was unmitigatedly angry now. Yes, even with Lucretia, whom everybody "bowed down to," herself as well. Lucretia had gone too far this time. She felt as if she always should be angry with her and did not wish to be any other way. She sat down at her room and thought over all the hateful things that had been said. Lucretia had made fun of her parlor furniture and she had as much as said she didn't treat Stephen's wife well, and said that other dreadful thing about her religion. Hadn't she trouble enough already but Lucretia must come and add to it? And she there on a visit, too, and hadn't seen her in so long! Why was it that everybody seemed to be down upon her lately? A wild wish passed through her mind that she could go out of life and be done with it forever.

"Go where?" The question came with startling force as if another had asked it. She was not ready, feeling as she did now, to step into the next world and in another second stand face-to-face with the Lord Jesus. She could feel how his eyes would be fixed upon her in sorrowful reproach with a look in them that Stephen's eyes had the other morning when she scolded about something Julia had done.

And then through all the tumult of her being, there

came that which comes once in a lifetime only to some—that swift revealing of herself to herself. A hateful picture, and she hated it with all her soul. With all the anger died out she recalled one thing her sister had said with keenest anguish. It was not that last thrust about the parlor not nor that she had been cross and unkind to her children but it was this—Lucretia had said that her religion did not help herself or anybody else. They were terrible words and they were true. She had attended to all outward duties and had not made her inner life sweet. She had been cross and ugly to her son's wife and Julia had borne it well. Sure enough she was a saint. "St. Julia." And Stephen, poor fellow—how unhappy she had made him all these months. The first year of his married life his mother had spoiled. But she would atone—she would. And there was Lucretia. She had probably been a stumbling block to her and kept her out of the kingdom. How could she ever be forgiven? There came a swift gracious answer to that question. Even as she had seen her wrongdoing with the light of eternity flashed over it, so now she was brought face to face with the pitying, loving Christ. She had no more doubt that she was forgiven than the child gathered in its mother's arms.

In the morning Mrs. Dale was surprised to find a strange tenderness of heart. She had expected after long struggles with herself she might in time come to regard her son's wife as she should, when lo! Here, without conflict, her feelings were all changed and she wished to love her and gain her love, her own past conduct seeming monstrous and wicked. And why was it strange after all? She had submitted, the rebellion was at an end. It was but to keep his own promise, "A right spirit will I put within you," and it was like himself to bestow forgiving love and plenteous grace. If other submissions were but were perfect he would oftener amaze us with a royal graciousness.

She read a few verses in her Bible that morning as one drinks cold water when thirsty. She had no time for Bible reading usually. It was one of the "weightier matters" that she had omitted.

"That ye put off concerning the former conversations the old man ... And that ye put on the new man which is after God created in righteousness and true holiness," she read. Yes, that was what she must do. "Put off the old" woman. Be a new woman and take for daily orders from her King these closing verses of the chapter:

"Let all bitterness, and wrath, and anger, and clamor, and evil speaking be put away from you, with all malice; and be ye kind one to another, even as God for Christ's sake hath forgiven you."

Aunt Crete looked curiously at her sister when she

came downstairs early and found her alone that morning. She half-expected that Maria would be "glum." What was her surprise when her sister came over to her and put her arms about her saying in a broken voice, "Lucretia, you were right, my religion didn't do me any good nor anybody else. I'm going to begin at the beginning again now and I want everybody to forgive me all the harm I've done."

Voluble Aunt Crete, who had never lacked a word before in her life, was mute now. She tried to speak but something choked her voice and dimmed her eyes. She could only press her sister's hand. Then the two grey heads came together and they kissed each other, which these matter-of-fact women never did except when they are parted.

Mrs. Dale was glad that her sister and their visitor went after breakfast to spend the day with another friend. She wanted time to think on this new day of her life. She had some large and important plans to perfect. Everything in that house was going to be different! She went into the parlor and shut the door to think it out. She sat down in one of the horsehair chairs, and tried it. Sure enough, it was slippery—she could even smile at a vision of Lucretia's ample proportions sliding down the cellar door. Why had she never noticed before that they were not comfortable?

The parlor and the children's room should have new furniture! She said "children" to herself for the first time, with a little exultant swell of her heart—and the parlor furniture should go to her own room. That in her room would be just something to give to Widow Barnes who lost everything in the fire. There should be a girl in the kitchen, and Julia and she would take turns superintending—and here she registered a remarkable vow for an old housekeeper. She would not by word or look interfere with Julia during her turn of managing, and she would not give advice unless asked.

Truly, Mrs. Dale's repentance was genuine. Her first thought was to write a long letter to Stephen and tell him everything. On second thought, she decided to live and change in her spirit instead of telling it, and let it be a surprise day by day, telling only what is necessary to carry out plans.

The next morning Stephen was amazed beyond measure to receive this most remarkable letter from his mother. He could scarcely believe his eyes as he read:

"Dear Stephen—I have decided to refurnish the parlor and the east room upstairs. Don't you ask any questions but just do as I tell you. Are you smart enough to get up a plan so that Julia could select them and not have the least idea who they are for? Let's have a Christmas surprise for her. Get everything that ought to go in a pretty parlor and bedroom and send them as soon as possible."

There was little more of it except some neighborhood news and an affectionate ending, nothing to explain her strange request.

Stephen was overjoyed. It was not like his mother to write out her feelings at length, but something had changed her, else why would she care to please Julia in the furnishing? The tone of her letter, too, was different, more like her old self. A great weight fell from his heart and he thanked God. It was not long either before a plan was afoot that should have his wife select the furniture and yet be none the wiser.

Consequently, Mrs. Stephen Dale was unsuspecting when one fine morning her sister, Mrs. Saybrook, came in dressed for shopping saying: "Julia, you love to buy pretty things, come and help me will you? My husband has a commission. A particular friend has asked as a great favor that he select certain articles of furniture for a young couple. He has deputized me, and I want you to choose them. What is the good of fine taste if you do not make it useful? On our way downtown we must make a memoranda. You think of the very prettiest way to furnish a parlor and large bedroom—not extravagantly, for refined people living in a large country town."

It was not in human nature to entirely repress a sigh of envy is the young wife selected carpet, furniture and portieres of sea green and gray with the sheerest of muslin draperies for windows. And then, all unaware, chose fair appointments for her own bedroom. It was done with painstaking detail and regard to matching in contrast, saying as she made the decisions:

"I am going to get everything as I would like it myself, but perhaps it won't please that other young woman."

And her sister, smiling, answered, "I know she would like them."

Stephen had been thinking much about his mother during his absence, and realized as he had not before that his marriage, somewhat sudden, must have come as a sort of shock to her. Then, to, she might often have been lonely, and possibly he had not been as thoughtful of her as he might have been, and—had he been cold to her of late? Dear mother, she was growing old; he might not have her many years longer. His heart smote him, and an eager wish arose to do some little things to prove to her that he thought of her pleasure at this Christmas tide which had always been much made of in their family. What if he should go home and spend Christmas with her—returning for Julia—and try to make it like one of their old-time happy days? When he proposed the plan to Julia she answered:

"Yes, I think you ought to go if you feel so; but can't I go, too? I want to be where you are, and it will only be shortening our visit a day or two. Besides I've been thinking a little myself. I might have done more to win your mother. I have a nice present to take to her and I'm going this new year to try to be to her just what I would like you to be to my mother, if we lived with her. Then, you know, it will not be like my giving up Christmas at home. We are all to spend the day at Aunt Laura's; a great crowd of uncles, aunts and cousins. They'll never miss me."

To her surprise Mrs. Dale received word that her son would reach home sooner than he had intended. Christmas Eve had come, with all in readiness, and Aunt Crete was on her way to the station to meet the travelers, but Mrs. Dale sat by the window looking out. Against the sunset sky was outlined the stone tower of the old church. From its quaint belfry now pealed out the evening chimes, the old-time carol:

"Peace on earth goodwill to men."

The sweet sounds stole in upon the calmed heart of

this mother like a benediction. Her uplifted spirit rejoiced in them. Peace had come to her, even the peace of God. Henceforth her life should be one long endeavor to be a coworker with him by promoting peace on earth. She could well sit in quiet content, waiting, for her lovely plans had been accomplished, and others added. The whole house had been re-papered and painted. And Aunt Crete, wise in worldly ways, had superintended the hanging of draperies and artistic arrangement of furniture.

"Now it looks ready to receive your pretty daughter," she told her sister as she took a last survey of the daintily appointed chamber, complete even to a single rose in a vase.

At first Stephen's wife noticed nothing except that her mother-in-law took her in her arms and kissed her— a genuine motherly kiss. Then she gazed about the beautiful room in bewilderment exclaiming, "Why!"

Aunt Crete interposed just here and carried them off to the east room—the big bear east room with staring walls and ugly carpet. Where was it?

This dream of beauty with delicate tints and soft white draperies had somehow a familiar look to Julia. Suddenly exclamations and interjections ended in a low cry of delight as she recognized her own purchases.

"Oh, Stephen!" she began. "No wonder you look so

beaming."

"Stephen had nothing to do with it except carrying out orders. Mother is the good fairy!" he said proudly, and radiant, as if his crowning joy comes now that his mother was shining forth so grandly.

The young wife divined it all. There was a look of love, even for her, in her mother-in-law's face. Their eyes met and the spiritual telegraphy was understood. Julia went over to her and clasped her close, murmuring, "Mother dear!"

"Maria, I don't mind telling you," Aunt Crete whispered to her sister as she bade her goodbye, "that I want to be a Christian myself since I seen you made over. I do believe in you, all three of you, and I want you to forgive me for hurting your feelings that day. I was ugly and cross-grained myself."

HAZEL CUNNINGHAM'S DENIAL

by

Grace Livingston Hill

(Originally published in 1902)

HAZEL CUNNINGHAM'S DENIAL

"Hazel, do you want to pack your Bible?"

"Why, certainly I do. Alice Cunningham, do you suppose I am going to put my religion away on the clothes-press shelf till I get back from my vacation?"

"Well, a good many people do, you'll find," answered her sister, laughing. "I don't believe you'll have much time where you are going to read it—not if it's anything as it was when I was there three years ago. There'll be boating and bathing in the surf, besides sailing on the river when you're not playing golf or tennis. Golf's the great thing down there. And then there'll be walks on the beach in the moonlight. By the way, Jean told me that Burton Channing is coming home from Europe and going to spend his entire summer down there. You'll be sure to meet him; he's a great golf player. They say he's on the links from morning to night. I almost envy you your summer. If I were not going to the mountains I could not resist going with you.

"Hazel!" called a voice from downstairs. "Is your trunk ready? I told the man to be here at twelve, and it's half-past eleven now."

"Almost!" answered Hazel, rising from her seat on the floor by her trunk, and hastily seizing a pile of shirt waists from the bed, she crammed the first tray down to make room for the second one. The Bible, in the rush that followed, was left lying under a gingham apron that Alice had thrown off hastily when she ran down to answer the doorbell a little later. And perhaps that was the whole trouble, for when one forgets one's Bible there is no telling what may happen.

Hazel Cunningham had been established almost a week in the wide, low farm-house with its broad piazzas and its many windows looking out upon the green velvet turf of the golf links and on down to the broad silver of the Manasquan River, flecked with many white sails. The little white-walled room with its simple furnishings and muslin curtains, even the high bureau and the tin candlestick, which held the only light the house supplied, seemed charming to her.

She had played golf every day for hours till her smooth, plump arms and well-rounded cheeks were browned from the sun's rays. And this beautiful Sunday morning she was lying still for a few minutes before arising, drinking in the sounds that came through the open windows; the soft twittering of the birds in the apple trees outside; the distant roar of the waves as they beat upon the sand at the beach, and the jingle of dishes in the distant kitchen. There was the wafting of a savory smell of breakfast, mingled with the perfume of mignonette in the old rowboat, that served as a flower-bed on the sea of green lawn. How beautiful it all was! Pretty soon she would get up and read in her Bible to begin this first Sunday aright, for she, poor child, had been so busy and so happy that she had not yet discovered the absence of her Bible. Then there would be church, and she planned which of her pretty gowns she would wear, and wondered how the service would be, there in a new church.

A gentle tap on the door aroused her, and one of the crowd of girls who made the farm-house ring with merriment, called through the key hole:

"Hazel, I just slipped up to tell you that Burton Channing arrived late last night. I thought you'd want to put on your best golf skirt. He'll be sure to be on the links this morning I should think, he's such an enthusiast. Hurry down, can't you?"

Hazel managed to make some reply, and her informant hurried down the hall to impart her information to another girl. But the girl whom she left was not the happy creature that she had been before her caller came. The astounding fact that these girls meant to play golf on Sunday, and that they expected her to do so also, was a shock to her.

She recollected that they had planned their games and frequently spoken of "tomorrow" the night before, but she had supposed, of course, they misspoke themselves and intended to say Monday. Indeed, last evening she had almost forgotten what the next was to be, they were all so merry. Could it be that they had all forgotten? No, for now she could remember also how they had spoken of this one and that who would be down on the late train to spend Sunday. No, they had not forgotten. And the worst of it was that they were girls who would not hesitate to laugh at her openly if she refused to play with them.

What could she do? Go to church and endure the fire of taunts that would be hers when she returned? Have Louise Blakely and Florence Whittington call her a little saint as they had done with Martha Worthington, who would not go sailing because her mother worried? There were circumstances under which the term "saint" might be a crown of glory to one, but not in the mouths of those two girls.

She shuddered and turned over in bed, feeling for the first time how hard the husk mattress was and how limp and small the pillows. No longer the sweet breeze called her, and no longer did the delicate odor from the kitchen stir her appetite. She was utterly miserable, foreseeing the ordeal through which she was about to pass and half-conscious of her own miserable failure.

Then, there was Burton Channing! She had never met him, but for the last five years since her sister had met him abroad she had heard his praises sounded until now it seemed nothing short of a catastrophe to miss making a good impression upon a young man who had it in his power to make life for her so enjoyable. What should she do? She never could go and play golf. Her upbringing had been very strict about the Sunday. What would her father and mother and sister think? Yes, and the church people at home?

Sad to say she had been away from her Bible so many days that she did not stop to ask herself what God would think of her. She lay still, trying to think what to do, and one by one she recognized the voices of the girls on the lawn below. Once she raised up on one elbow and pulled back the curtain just a little. Yes, they were all in full golf costume, just as on week days, only a little more dainty than usual. Fine white shirt waists, some of the sleeves rolled to the elbow, the glimmer of a brilliant red jacket, the poise of a pretty low shoe! They all represented to Hazel the life she had been living during the past week, and which her conscience cried out against for today, and yet which she had not the courage to abjure.

They came in search of her after a time, knocking loudly and demanding to come in, and she pleaded sleepiness and a headache and shook them off. The breakfast hour passed, and they clamored for her again, and there was nothing for a coward like Hazel but to take refuge in the headache.

"It isn't like her a bit," they said as they started off reluctantly without her, their bundle of golf-sticks slung over their shoulders. "She never has a headache, and always seems so well and strong. And I never thought she was lazy."

Hazel thought to get up and slip off unseen to church by herself, but the voices below warned her that all were not gone away from the house, and looking down again she saw the two she dreaded most, Louise Blakely and Florence Whittington, lounging in the hammock under the big apple tree with novels and a box of chocolates.

Distant bells were chiming with the dashing of the surf, while a group of people were walking down the avenue of oaks to church, and others were climbing into the big omnibus—for the beach perhaps. A fine-looking young man—at least his shoulders were fine—was holding a parasol over an elderly woman. He took her Bible from her and carried it under his arm. They were evidently going to church and must have come in late last night, for they were strangers. How she wished she were on the way to church with them!

With a groan she plunged back into the pillow again and cried, so that when the golf players returned at noon and found her on the piazza in a white muslin dress, her heavy eyes made good her morning's story of a headache, and they inquired sympathetically after her.

The visitor of the early morning sat down beside and essayed to offer comfort:

"Mr. Channing didn't come out this morning after all, Haze. He must have overslept after his journey. But he'll be sure to be there this afternoon. You can walk down after dinner under my big white umbrella, can't you? The playing was fine this morning. You ought to have seen George. He got there in great shape, I tell you."

Poor bewildered Hazel listened to their talk and did not join in. How interesting it would have been to her another day! And here it was Sunday, and not a word from beginning to end was said that would let anyone know the day was recognized. No thought of church, of sermon or text—not even a criticism.

After dinner the others would not take no for an answer. They carried Hazel off by storm to the golf links, established her under a tree with cushions and a wide umbrella, and two or three willing young men to keep her company, and she spent a gay afternoon still more miserable than her morning had been.

It was almost suppertime when she was at last on her way back to the house. She felt she would breathe freer when the day was past. Mr. Channing had not come to the links at all. She was savagely glad for that. Her conscience was loudly accusing her. She was remembering that at home it would be almost time to start for the young people's evening meeting at the church. Her thoughts were so preoccupied that she scarcely noticed a group by the piazza until they were close upon them, and then she looked up to recognize the broad shoulders of the young man who took his mother to church that morning, and almost immediately someone introduced them. It was Burton Channing!

A flood of color rushed under the tan, which she could not control. Had he seen her come from the golf links? How thankful she was that she did not wear her short skirt as the others did, for he had not been ashamed to go to church with his mother; no, nor to carry a Bible. How was it that she had judged that just because he had spent several years abroad that he would despise her for keeping the Sabbath? And what was this he was saying—kindly, unostentatiously, but frankly:

"No, Miss Whittington, I don't play on Sunday. I

was at church this morning. But I think it will be a good day tomorrow for the links."

"Oh, dear me! I didn't know you were so awfully good, Mr. Channing," said Miss Whittington. "We shall all have to go to church now you've come, I suppose, and it's such a bore," and she pouted prettily.

Was it chance that Hazel's eyes met those of the young man as he answered pleasantly:

"I hope you all will. Tonight will be a good time to begin. There's to be a beach meeting and a friend of mine from China is going to speak. You'll not be bored by him, I know."

Hazel Cunningham felt like a veritable hypocrite for receiving and returning that look of understanding he gave her. She knew she had not been true to her conscience. She felt that he did not take her for one of the rest. She was not sure whether she was most glad or ashamed about it.

She slipped away from the supper table before the rest and dressed to go to the meeting. The other girls would probably say that she was going on account of the young man's presence and invitation; but they were all doing that, and it was just punishment for the cowardly way in which she had acted that morning. Before she left the little white room she kneeled beside her bed and asked to be forgiven, and to be allowed to undo the wrong she had done that day. Then she went softly downstairs, while the rest were getting ready to go, changing golf suits for fluffy white and pink and blue draperies.

As Hazel crossed the piazza Burton Channing rose from one of the rockers.

"Are you going to the beach meeting, Miss Cunningham?" he said. "And may I walk with you? Mother does not feel rested enough to go tonight. I have met your sister, you know, and that ought to make us old friends."

They were walking down the arch of oaks now, and Hazel was dimly conscious of jealous eyes upon her from the many-windowed farm-house. But the next words of her companion put all such thoughts to flight.

"I have heard a great deal about you, you know, and the minute I saw you I knew I had found a kindred spirit. Among all these Sabbath-breakers a simple, honest, Christian feels a little lonesome now and then. I must confess I was pleased this afternoon to see you did not wear the regulation short skirt and rolled-up sleeves today. Isn't it strange how people can be so indifferent about Sunday?"

Hazel's face was fairly burning now, and for the instant she was tempted to cover her first cowardice with a second. She had but to keep still and agree with him and he would be none the wiser as to her weakness, but something in her cried out against herself, and with almost tears in her eyes she told him what a miserable day she had spent.

It was all so humiliating and different from the way she had planned this first meeting with the much-talked-of young man. And yet as she sat on the beach while the wonderful singing rolled all about her, blending with the anthem of the sea, and remembered his quick sympathy and the little story he had told her of his own first testing time and failure, and how easily he had made her see that she had been thinking more of what others would say than of her Master, she was glad that God in his tenderness had led her just as he had done.

As her heart joined in the prayer and singing, thrilling with the words of the speaker, and feeling God's presence in the sound of wind and wave, she felt she could never meet temptation again quite so much off her guard, for it was as if her Father spoke to her and showed her how she had sinned against his love.

FAITH AND LOVE

PROFESSOR KENDRICK'S DISCOVERIES

by

Marcia Livingston

(Originally published in 1893)

PROFESSOR KENDRICK'S DISCOVERIES

The village of Woodland was astir in an unusual manner one summer morning. Groups of men and boys gathered on the square at an early hour. Work-a-day attire was laid aside; young girls and children flitted about in white dresses and bright ribbons, while gay little flags fluttered from the houses.

The birthday of our national independence was to be celebrated in an appropriate manner. Among other attractions promised was a balloon ascension; not a toy affair, but a real vehicle for navigating the air, and a real traveler in it. It had been talked of for days in the little town—the immense balloon, and the bravery of the man who was to undertake so perilous a journey. Speculations as to the state of things above the clouds and the recital of hair-breadth escapes by aeronauts had filled the minds of the loungers at the corner grocery, as well as the more respectable men who were want to gather on the porch of Squire Lewis's law office, until all were in a state of expectancy.

Trim white houses faced the long shaded street. On

the lawn of one of these two little girls of four and six frolicked with their kitten, occasionally running to an old gentleman who sat on the veranda reading his newspaper, to ask, "Grandpa, isn't it 'most time for the b'loon to go up?"

Grandpa at last folded up his newspaper and put on his hat. Dorrie and Dee were at his side in an instant grasping the skirts of his coat.

"These fidgets can't wait any longer," he told his daughter-in-law, who came out just then, "so we'll jog on. You and John had better start soon, or you will miss it, for I think they must be almost ready by this time."

The mother glanced over the children to see that they were in order, weighing the question for an instant whether or not they needed their jackets, and deciding that as the day was warm they did not, so she watched them go down the street, each with a chubby hand clasped in grandpa's, the brown curls and the gold curls glancing in the sunshine. Then she turned away with a satisfied feeling that they were in safe care, for Mrs. Reynolds was one of those mothers who possess vivid imaginations and sensitive nerves, and in consequence suffered fear and torment lest some evil should come to her darlings when they were out of her sight. She felt at ease, though, when grandpa had them. He was so cautious and wise, and loved them so dearly, being one of the few privileged persons who could carry them off without numberless charges.

And so the young mother went singing about her work with gladness of heart little knowing—Who does?—what the next hour should bring to her.

Grandpa pushed his way through the crowd after laying in a stock of oranges and candy, to get a near view of the ship which was to sail through the air. It would soon be off now as the preparations were nearly completed.

"Oh, what a pretty place!" Dorrie said, peeping into the basket of the balloon. "Grandpa, let us get in just a minute, please, won't you?"

"Pease do," chimed in Dee's sweet voice.

Grandpa never denied any request of his pets that lay within the range of possibility. He hesitated a little, then assuring himself that there could be no danger, just for a moment, he lifted them in. No sooner were they seated, and looking about them, with delight than, by somebody's mismanagement, in an awful second of time, the huge monster broke its bonds and shot unbidden into the air. It was a fearful moment. The few who knew of the precious burden it carried sent up a wailing cry of distress. The grandfather stood, horror-stricken, confounded, gazing after it, then rushed wildly about calling for help. But help there was none. Even the master and creator of the wonderful thing sailing majestically through the air stood powerless, watching it steadily mount on its upward way.

Into this scene came the father and mother of the children. They had been strolling along in a leisurely way, but quickened their steps as they saw the balloon ascend. They watched its swift smooth motion with delighted eyes, George Reynolds explaining to his wife its mechanism and estimating its rate of speed.

Suddenly they become aware that people were looking at them in a strange way, and then their father came towards them with white face and tottering gate. He opened his lips to speak, but no sound came out. The pitying neighbors gathered about, and one, as gently as he could, told the terrible news. The mother's swift intuitions had half divined the truth, that her children were in peril, as soon as she saw their grandfathers grief-stricken face.

"Are they alone?" she gasped, as the awful words fell like blows upon her heart. The man silently bowed his head.

For an instant she fell back into her husband's arms, and a deathly paleness overspread her face; then, controlling herself by a great effort, she lifted her head and searched the sky for that fearful object which was bearing her darlings on and up above the clouds into that mysterious ocean of space where mortal eyes could not follow and mortal hands could not reach. Not now must she give way to weakness and faintness. She would never lose sight of it while it was visible. And the whole multitude, awed into solemn silence, stood and watched with her, save a band of brave men who sprang up, mounted swift horses, and hurried away in the direction the balloon had taken, assuring George Reynolds as they went that, if it were possible, the children should be rescued, begging him, meantime, to stay with his wife.

The grandfather had buried his face in his hands, and sunk down in a stupor of grief. It was but for a moment, though. He roused himself, and securing a horse, mounted and followed the others. His son came to his side as he was starting, and pleaded:

"Oh, father, don't go! You are not able. I will go. You stay with Mary; do, father."

"I have to go," the old man said, with set lips. "I shall die staying here to wait," and he went, distancing all the others.

The son watched him ride away, his gray locks streaming in the breeze, his eyes flashing, all traces of the weakness of age vanished, and every muscle strained and tense, as if the fire of youth had returned to him. Even the horse seemed to have caught the eager intensity of his spirit, and fairly flew over the ground.

George Reynolds longed to follow him, but a glance at his wife's white face decided him to stay by her side.

The agony of suspense was almost intolerable, as they watched the balloon almost touched the trees on the hilltops, then hover over the waters of the lake. They held their breaths as it seemed to be descending into its dark waters. Oh! Would it a light there? But no, it rose again and soared away higher and higher above the clouds. Now it began to grow smaller and dimmer; then a mere speck, and, at last, strain their eyes as they would, they could not find it. The little ones were adrift, alone on a sea of air, and a pall of sorrow had been thrown over the village which a short time before hummed with joyous life.

The husband and wife looked into each other's faces without speaking, and, silently, hand in hand, went home, where not even the kindest neighbors dared intrude upon their peculiar sorrow. The tea table had been made ready before Mrs. Reynolds left home. Two chairs, higher than the others, with bibs hanging over them, were placed at the table before two gay little plates. There was a pink mug beside one plate, and a blue one by the other. A few hours ago that house was full and happy, now it was empty, desolate and horrible. Objects on every side mocked them. There was Dee's torn little sun hat thrown down where she had left it. Dorrie's doll set upright in a toy chair, and a handful of wilted buttercups lay on the porch. Night was coming on, and two little beds were empty. Where were their darlings? Were they still up in that clear sky or dashed to pieces on the earth?

Mary Reynolds had reason to be thankful that night that a man so strong and tender and full of faith was her husband. While she walked the floor in a state bordering on insanity, with eyes distended and tearless, and each breath an involuntary groan, he, fearing the worst for her, assumed a composure he did not feel, and set about doing little things for her comfort. He kindled the fire and made the tea, and forced himself to speak cheerfully, saying they would doubtless hear of their darlings in a short time. With the effort to cheer her, his own distracted heart grew calmer.

After they had gone through the semblance of a meal, Mrs. Reynolds begged her husband to take the horse and buggy and they, too, would start out and join the march—it would be so much more endurable than waiting at home.

"But Mary," he answered, "don't you know that nearly all the men in the village are out at different points? They are to send reports here whenever they have any, so we shall probably get the news sooner if we stay at home than if we go wandering about. I fear, too, you could not bear the strain of such a thing. We can pray. The Lord has promised to hear those who pray in faith. He is perfectly able to take care of our children, and bring them back to us whatever their danger. Now let us trust him absolutely."

With the spoken prayer of agonizing importunity and yet of child-like submission, the mother's heart grew calmer and the saving tears started.

Through the long, long hours they watched and prayed and listened for the footsteps of those who should bring them tidings, at times mounting up on wings of faith and hope and again sinking into despair. Sometimes they went to one of the upper windows, and standing hand-in-hand, searched the sky, each being too pitiful to speak to the other their secret thoughts, which, if spoken, would have been:

"How strange to be standing at the attic window after midnight, looking up into the far-away skies for our darlings."

But search as they might with keenest gaze that cruel, cloudless, moonlight sky, no speck appeared in all the sea of air.

Once a messenger came to say—all in one breath, and then to hasten away—that when the moon arose, they could discern the balloon, though very far off. Their darlings were still safe then, unless they had died of terror or cold. The mother recollected with a pang that two warm sacks hung in the closet, and that thin muslin only covered the dear little arms.

The young aeronauts who were the occasion of so much distress shouted with glee when they found themselves in motion. But as they rose higher above the houses and trees, little Dee's eyes grew wide with fear, and she cried, "Take me out! I want to get out!"

"Oh, take care, you will fall out!" cried the elder sister. "Don't be a baby, Dee. This is a bu'ful ride. Why, we're flying!" And the child who was born destitute of fear, drew a long breath of delight, doubtless feeling something of the joyous sense of freedom known to a bird on the wing.

"I don't want to go up in the sky," said Dee, with grieved curling lip. "I'm 'fraid!"

"Why, maybe will go way up to God's house," Dorrie said, with large excited eyes. "Won't that be nice!"

"I want to go home," wailed Dee. "I want my suppy." And then as the greatest of all needs searched over her, began to cry and earnest and moan out, "I want my mama!"

"Don't cry, dearie," Dorrie said, wiping the tears from her sister's face. "Jesus will take care of us. And pretty soon, maybe, perhaps we'll get a nice big house and supper'll be all ready, 'nen we'll eat supper, 'nen we'll go to bed, and in the morning a nice man will take us home in his horse and buggy, and mama will be standing at the gate to meet us," declared the little woman of with vivid imagination and beautiful faith.

"I'm 'fraid. I—I want mama *now*," sobbed the poor baby.

"Now, listen," the wise little woman went on. "I'll tell you what we will do. We will go to sleep, and when we wake up we'll be there! Won't that be nice? First we will say our prayers."

With clasped hands and bowed heads they lisped out, "Now I lay me," then Dorrie added, "Dear Jesus, please take care of us, 'cause we'm way up in the sky all 'lone, and we'm glad 'cause we know you will. Amen."

Did the Father listen and smile and answer, by sending a strong angel to "fly swiftly" and guide his little saints through the trackless space?

The prayer ended, the babies' eyes closed in sleep, while their father and mother prayed on, and all the mothers in the village who were acquainted with God watched and prayed. And to the dear old man, who pursued with feverish haste that dim object in the sky, his every breath was a prayer.

That same evening, in a quiet picturesque town nearly a hundred miles away, Elizabeth Dorset sat on the porch after tea, reading the newspaper to her father. It was a peaceful home in the quaint old house which had sheltered many generations of Dorsets. For years the lives of the old people had flowed evenly along, ministered to by Elizabeth, best of daughters, bright, energetic and sweet-spirited, not at all looking her thirty years, with clear gray eyes, straight brows, and a mouth that could be both loving and firm. The old father and mother thanked God for her that night as she sat in a low chair with the setting sunlight turning her brown hair into gold; thanked Him, that although she had passed through trials, she had come out of them into these calm and happy days.

Elizabeth had her story. At twenty her idol proved to be clay of the commonest sort. Her heart had been sore for a time, almost rebellious indeed; but during these last years, with finer discernment and higher standards of manly character, she had become content, and even glad, that her early dreams had never been realized. The experience had not rendered her cynical, although she privately cherished the conviction that all men of noble aims and staunch integrity were extinct, except it might be her father and grandfather and a few others well in years.

After Elizabeth had gone through the *Tribune*, making her father acquainted with the state of affairs in foreign countries, besides politics and news in general at home, she was accustomed to forage over it for choice bits suited to her own tastes. She found it that evening, and the announcement of a new comet to make its first appearance in the heavens between the hours of one and two, July 4, visible at first in the southeast.

"And this is the very night, father," Elizabeth said with more excitement than she was wont to manifest.

"And the southeast is there," the old man answered, pointing it out, "just behind Wintergreen Hill. The barn is in the way; we should have to go to the front of the garden likely, to see it when it first appears."

"Let's go, father," the daughter said, with a face that had in it the eagerness of a child.

"I'm astonished that you, 'Lizabeth, wanting your father to go poking about in the middle of the night at this time of life, losing his sleep—and you, too, when tomorrow's ironing day. You would feel like wilted cabbage leaves in the morning. I guess you won't do any such thing."

The actual ruler of the small household had spoken now, practical, resolute Mrs. Dorset, whose ample proportions filled the rocking chair at the other end of the porch, the click of her needles keeping time with the swaying of her chair. There was a frown on her benevolent face, as she uttered these arbitrary sentences, which father and daughter heeded. Nevertheless, good Mrs. Dorset was oblivious of the fact that she was, on a small scale, a tyrant. She did not intend to be so; she simply had a desire to have everything move along smoothly and orderly in the accustomed grooves; and in general she managed well; the subjugated ones, from long habit, usually submitted with a good grace, never admitting, except to their very secret souls, that there was the slightest compulsion in the matter, or that the peace of the household required it.

"I have not seen a comet, you know, since I was a very little girl," Elizabeth said, bringing out an old astronomy book and an encyclopedia to investigate the subject further. The more she studied and thought about it the more wonderful did it appear and the stronger was her desire to see the mysterious visitant slowly emerge into view from behind the hill, so that, by bedtime, she had formed a half-guilty purpose to steal out by herself and enjoy the rare pleasure. Why should she not do so innocent a thing, she told herself in vindication. She was a woman with rights, even though her mother had not discovered it, and yet, dear mother, she would not go contrary to her wishes for the world. But this was so small a thing and so innocent, and mother need never be the wiser.

The old farmhouse had taken on its slumbers air by nine o'clock. Elizabeth, her resolution taken and plans made, lay down on the outside of her bed, her watch by her side and the light burning dimly, feeling as much nervous trepidation, she told herself, as if she were about to abscond to parts unknown, instead of to the lower end of the garden.

Amidst confusing dreams she heard the old clock toll out, in a sepulchral tone, the hour of one. She rose quickly, and throwing on a long cloak and a fleecy white thing over her head, stepped out into the back hall. Going down the front stairs and opening the front door was not to be thought of; she would surely disturb her father and mother. The backstairs served the purpose nicely, as they led into the woodshed, remote from their rooms. And yet as she stole down them, and they creaked under her weight, as stairs always do under a stealthy tread, she half-expected to hear her mother call out:

"Is that you 'Lizabeth? What's the matter?"

She was safely down at last, and in the grass where her tread was noiseless.

It was with a strange sense of freedom and exultation

that she looked about her that summer moonlit night, as she walked with glad springing step. How good it was to be alone for once out in the night, nobody awake but herself in all the village. She might run and jump is when she was a child, and no curious eyes would be upon her, and, suiting the action to the thought, this young woman ran swiftly down the hill. How delightful to have the monotony of her prosaic life varied by standing alone in the dead of night, in the silence and sweetness of the dewy garden, fragrant with roses and balmy with the breath of sweet-briar and rosemary. Who knew before that the old garden was such an enchanted place as it seems now with soft lights and weird shadows!

As she reached the fence she almost screamed in surprise and terror, for, leaning against a tree, but a few feet away from her, stood a man! Her first impulse was to run back as fast as her feet could carry her, but another look changed her mind. How foolish she had been! It was Dr. Vaile of course, her own pastor, whose garden joined theirs. He had probably come out on the same errand as herself.

"Dr. Vaile," she called. "Have you found the comet?"

The man turned, and came near lifting his hat. Horrors! It was not Dr. Vaile's gray-bearded face which came to view! This man was a stranger, with smooth face, square chin, and keen eyes; not a young man nor yet a middle-aged man. Even in that hasty glance Elizabeth saw that it was a scholarly, refined face, and on that account was not absolutely terror-stricken.

"I am not Dr. Vaile," he said courteously. "I am only his cousin, John Kendrick. I arrived but this evening, and am out prospecting for the new comet. You are Dr. Vaile's neighbor?"

"Yes, Elizabeth Dorset," the young woman answered with simple dignity, and her fears vanished; she had often heard Mrs. Vaile speak of their cousin, Professor Kendrick of the university.

"I have a small telescope here, Miss Dorset," he said, "and when the comet appears we shall be able to have a good view of it from this point, I think."

Elizabeth hesitated. She would give anything to have a look through that telescope. What was the right thing to do? How shocked all Woodville would be if it were reported that Elizabeth Dorset held interviews in the back garden with a stranger in the dead of night. She heartily wished just then that Dame Rumor would mind her own affairs, as does many another innocent woman who knows that there really can be no objection to the thing she desires to do, except this—that the tongue of said dame would wag to her detriment.

Elizabeth was spared making a decision, however, by

a most un-looked-for occurrence. There appeared at that instant in the sky to which the gaze of both was directed, a remarkable sight—not the comet, but a large dark object which came rapidly nearer, circling about above their heads, and finally settled in the top of the large tree, a few yards away.

"A balloon," exclaimed Professor Kendrick. "Can it be possible that anyone is in it?"

"I saw several notices for balloon ascensions for the Fourth. A woman was to ascend in one and Professor somebody," Elizabeth said, her voice tremulous with excitement.

They drew nearer to the tree, watching and listening, but neither saw nor heard signs of life. They were about to turn away when a faint sound like one murmuring in sleep caught the ears of each. They gazed at one another with astonished eyes.

"It sounded like a child's voice," whispered Elizabeth.

Hastily divesting himself of hat and coat, Professor Kendrick put in practice a long unused accomplishment of his boyhood, and nimbly climbed the branches, until he could look into the basket which rested firmly on the bows as if secured there by much effort. Amazement held him spell-bound for an instant.

"Two babies as I live!" he exclaimed, touching the warm cheek of one to make sure they were not made of wax, while scraps of heathen mythology and half-forgotten theories about angels floated vaguely through his brain as explanation of this strange sight. The moonbeams filtered through the leaves making dancing shadows over the white dresses of the little ones, lighting up their faces as they lay with arms about each other locked in sleep.

Dorrie, with little motherly care, had done what she could to shield her younger sister from the chill night air. Two scraps of handkerchiefs were spread over Dee's shoulders and fastened to her dress by a pin, these being the only resources at command.

"Pretty darlings!" The professor murmured, with misty eyes, and then, remembering that his thoughts must take more practical shape if he would rescue them, descended and took hasty counsel with the young woman who waited at the foot of the tree.

They canvassed the question thoroughly whether to remain where they were till morning and set up a watch over them, or to waken them and bring them down, or attempt to bring them down while sleeping. It was a perplexing situation even for two very bright people.

"If they are like most children in a sound sleep, it will be next to impossible to waken them so that they will have a grain of sense. And how could you bring them down while sleeping? They would be heavy as logs,"

Elizabeth said at last, casting a perplexed glance at the rather slender man before her.

"And yet, that seems the only thing to be done," the professor said, measuring the distance again with his eye. "If I had a ladder—but I dare not leave them long, they may fall."

"Come, I will show you where there is one," and Elizabeth ran like a deer through the garden path, the professor following in long strides. While he secured the ladder she went up to her room for blankets.

It seemed to Elizabeth, as she stood with fast-beating heart at the foot of the ladder placed firmly against the broad tree trunk, an almost impossible undertaking to hope to bring the children down in safety. And yet as she watched the agile man who, thanks to being an excellent gymnast, stepped easily and with sure footing from limb to limb, her courage revived. She shut her eyes for a moment as he appeared in sight with one of the children under his arm. If he should drop the child or make a false step! It was fearful! Her eyes would open and watch every movement. There was a dreadful fascination about it. Once the dress of the child caught on the sharp end of a broken branch, and she held her breath while it was being set free. Then a limb snapped and became unsafe. Her heart stood still while the brave man with one free hand reached to a strong branch above him, and swung himself and his precious burden to a sure place.

Ah! He was on the ladder now, almost down, and Elizabeth reached out her arms for the chubby form of little Dee. The blanket was spread on the ground, ready to receive her; she nestled down in it, and slept on safe.

"Blessed sleep of childhood!" exclaimed Professor Kendrick. "If she had awakened and struggled it would have gone hard with us."

Just a moment he rested, then he climbed the ladder again, and again Elizabeth stood silently watching his perilous descent, more difficult this time. Not only was Dorrie taller and heavier than her sister, but she was not so sound a sleeper. Perhaps, in his anxiety to secure a firm hold, her rescuer grasped her more tightly than he was aware. As he took a long step to the first reliable limb, she awoke and cried out: "Stop!" And then made a desperate effort to free herself. The professor did stop, and braced himself firmly against the strong branches. Then Dorrie heard a pleasant voice say: "Wake up, little girl. Do you know where you are?"

A pair of wide open eyes searched his face, as well as they could by glimmers of moonlight.

"Do you remember you took a ride in a balloon," the kind voice went on, "and it got dark, and you wanted to go home? Well, you fell asleep and your balloon sat down on a tree. I found you, and am carrying you down, and when morning comes I will take you home. If you are good and do just as I tell you, you will not be hurt."

"Where is Dee?" shrieked Dorrie, now awake to the situation.

"She is safely down there on the grass. A nice lady is taking care of her. Now, you will you be a good, brave girl, and keep very still while I take you down?"

"Yes, I will," said Dorrie, emphasizing her words by clinging so tightly to her preserver's neck that he was in danger of strangling.

"That's good. Hold fast now and we shall be all right."

With careful steps he clambered down. The child was as good as her word; she clung tightly, and no sound escaped her, even when her waving hair caught in a twig and received a smart pull.

The other rescuer stood with strained nerves and baited breath intently watching. "Thank God!" she exclaimed, as she received the other little stranger in her arms and wrapped the blanket about the shivering little form.

"Amen!" said the professor, with a long sigh of relief. "This little girl behaved nobly," he added, "or it might not have turned out so well. She is a brave child."

"And you are a brave man," Elizabeth wished to say; but she did not except in one admiring glance.

"What is our next duty, Miss Dorset?"

"To put these dear children to bed," said Elizabeth. "I think I can manage that by myself, for you must be sadly in need of rest by this time.

"I intend, by your leave, to see this job through to the end," he answered, stooping and lifting the sleeping Dee. "If you will lead the way with this other little woman we will follow."

The narrow back stairs were not to be thought of in this emergency, even if father and mother should waken, so Elizabeth left the party on the porch while she went through the woodshed to open the front door and strike a light. She did not speak one word to enjoin silence, but the professor took in the situation and tiptoed softly up the stairs.

It was a large, old-fashioned chamber into which Elizabeth led the way with high-posted bed and dainty white draperies, a quaint, delightful room, Professor Kendrick thought, in the hasty glance he could give it. He deposited his sleeping burden on the lounge, said that he would call in a few hours to learn more about the little travelers, then touched his hat, and with a "Good morning," was gone.

Elizabeth, wise woman that she was, asked no questions of Dorrie, who was in a half-dazed state from fatigue and disturbed slumbers, but gave her a cup of bread and milk and put her to bed in the shortest possible time. As Elizabeth laid herself down again she could but smile at the thought that her father and mother were apparently still oblivious of all she had passed through since she bade them "Good night."

The comet, meanwhile, despite the fact that it had been neglected and forgotten—for what is a sight of the very grandest heavenly body when too little earthly bodies are in peril?—now trailed itself in luminous beauty through the clear sky. Tired as he was, the enthusiastic scientist could not deny himself one long look through the telescope at the glorious visitor.

The first sound that Elizabeth heard next morning was her mother's voice at the foot of the stairs calling: "Elizabeth! Is anything the matter?"

"No, not now," came drowsily from the suddenly aroused sleeper.

"Not now—have you been sick in the night?"

"Oh, no, mother. I'll be down in a few minutes. Is it late?"

"It's going on to eight o'clock and Hannah's got breakfast on the table."

Mrs. Dorset could not remember the time when her

daughter Elizabeth had not been up early, bustling about, throwing open doors and windows, supervising breakfast, picking flowers for the table, and making the morning bright with her happy smile and fragment of song. What could have happened to her? Mrs. Dorset's voice actually trembled when she called her.

Elizabeth, when she did make her appearance, decided to defer the story of her night adventures till after breakfast, but her mother's experienced eyes, so accustomed to studying her idol's face, detected something there that puzzled her. There was a slight exhilaration in eye and tone, and a hint in them that she knew something she was not sharing with others— though Mrs. Dorset would not have thought of putting it in that way.

"'Lizabeth," said her mother, as she handed her a cup of coffee, "you look exactly as if you had been to Europe and knew a lot of things you are aching to tell about. What's the matter with you?" Then the old father bent a scrutinizing look upon his daughter from under shaggy brows, and Elizabeth laughed.

"What bright people my father and mother are," she said. "If I ever should have a secret, you would see straight through it at once. I thought I would not tell you till after breakfast, but it will have to come out. What do you say to my having to little travelers fast asleep in the east chamber?"

It was just as Elizabeth thought it would be: there was very little eating done while she told the wonderful story. No sooner had she finished then Mrs. Dorset, all excitement, left her second cup of coffee untasted and climbed the stairs to straightaway get a peep at the little sleepers.

"They're pretty creatures," she said, when she came down. "I wish we could keep them. But what a way their mother must be in by this time."

"Word must be sent at once," said Father Dorset.

"And they must be waked up right away, so that something can be found out," Mrs. Dorset exclaimed with energy.

Elizabeth hurried upstairs to attend to that duty herself. She had her own ideas about the matter of accomplishing it. She could not bring herself to waken them abruptly, so she opened the blinds and let the sunshine stream in. The song of the robin in the apple tree was contagious, and Elizabeth joined her voice to it in a merry ditty, such as children love. Intent on watching the robin she did not observe that Dorrie had awakened and was resting on her elbow gazing wonderingly about her.

The white room, the sunshine, the songs and the lady in light blue morning gown, with fine profile outlined on the curtain, made a fair picture to the beauty-loving child, and mingled with confused recollections of the night before, led to but one conclusion—they had reached heaven and this was a blue-robed angel!

Elizabeth was startled to hear a childish voice ask in half-whispered tones: "Is this God's house?"

She turned her head, prepared to see a sleepy looking child, but instead the little face expressed wonder, trust, rapture.

"Have we truly got there?" And the blue eyes searched her face with an eager look.

"Got where, dear?" Elizabeth asked, coming over to her.

"To heaven," said Dorrie.

The tears sprang to Elizabeth's eyes as she put her arms about the child. "No, dear, this is not heaven yet. It is only Mr. Dorset's house—some people who are going to heaven one day."

"Oh!" exclaimed Dorrie, looking dazed and disappointed.

"Don't you know we found you and your little sister in a balloon in the top of the tree last night? And a good man went up and brought you down and I put you to bed."

"And gave me bread and milk. Yes, I 'member," and a flash of recollection came to her face.

The child now thoroughly awake to all that had happened, was able to give a lucid account of the affair, together with the location of her home, her father's name in full, and everything necessary to ensure her safe return, much to Elizabeth's relief.

Little Dee, too, opened her brown eyes at last, and looked in a bewildered way about her. It took much explanation from her elder sister to make matters clear.

"I thought," said Dorrie, "when I woke up that we had got to heaven, but we didn't. Don't you know, dear Dee, I told you God would take care of us, and maybe he'd bring us to a nice big house, an' they'd give us some supper, an' put us to bed, an' we did that, an' they did, an' we're here."

"An' that's better'n heaven," sighed earthly Dee, stretching her chubby limbs in a yawn.

When Mary Reynolds stepped out on the porch that summer morning after a night of suspense and agony, the sunshine seemed to her cruel and mocking. She wondered how she could have felt so great interest yesterday in the bursting buds of a rosebush she had been nursing with care. They smiled up into her face this morning, half-blown in full bloom, the perfection of beauty, but they received no loving glance; her eyes were anxiously scanning the street, hoping and fearing that each footfall would prove to be that of a messenger with tidings, and yet the wild despair of the night before had passed away. She had even attained to a good degree of calmness and submission. Such is the strange, uplifting, overcoming strength imparted in answer to prayer; without it she must have died or lost her reason.

At last her eager watch was rewarded. The gate latch clicked, steps came up the walk, and she held in her hand a telegram which she dared not open. Her husband took it and broke the seal while she waited for the fateful words with clenched hands and labored breath. Presently his low-spoken, "Bless the Lord!" fell upon her ears like balm upon a wound, and he read:

"Children safe. Will arrive on 5:50 p.m. train. John Kendrick."

As prayer was the only relief to their hearts when heavy with grief, so now was there no outlet to the joy that surged over them except to kneel together and give thanks and praise to him who was all power in heaven and on earth—"and *between* heaven and earth," George Reynolds added.

The happy mother forgot weariness and want of sleep, and moved about her house with a light step in a lighter heart. She wondered how she could ever have thought the dining room too small or the kitchen not convenient. She had even murmured secretly sometimes that her lot was so commonplace and monotonous. Never again would she be guilty of so great ingratitude. How blessed her lot. How lovely her home, and what wonderful loving-kindness of the heavenly father to save as by a miracle their dear ones from a terrible death!

"Oh, my God, if it be thy will, spirit the dear lambs. Let me not be there murderer. Take me if thou wilt, old and worthless, but spare the babies."

This was the prayer of the old grandfather many times repeated through that dreadful night. At first he had ridden wildly and traveled weary miles aimlessly; but he bethought himself that there was One who knew the way perfectly. Why not ask Him as if He were traveling by his side? After that when he came to a turn in the road he would stop while he prayed to be guided in the right direction, adding to his pleading a pitiful petition: "If I might be the one to take them home dear Lord, oh, if I might!" And God, who has special kindnesses for old people and children, granted his request.

As he was passing through a town faint and weary

hearted, hope gone from him, he heard the joyful news of the children's rescue. Already a report of the thrilling incident had flashed through the country and stirred eager sympathies. Joy is as impatient of delay as suspense. Old Mr. Reynolds resolved to travel home in the swiftest possible way, so making arrangements to have his horse sent, he waited eagerly for the afternoon express which was nearly due. As it steamed in and he hastened to go on board, there came up to him from a car window a sweet voice chiming out: "There's gonpa!"

It could be none other voice then Dee's! Then Dorrie rushed to the window and called him in an ecstasy of joy. Never had the old man heard sweeter music. The next instant he held them both in his arms.

"Oh, sir!" he said at last to Professor Kendrick, who had the little ones in charge, and who had rehearsed the story of the rescue at least three times in reply to the old man's eager questions. "How can I show you my gratitude? I will serve you if ever you need it, even to giving up my life."

But Professor Kendrick assured him it was nothing but what anybody might have done, and that the credit was not due to him alone; he could not have succeeded so well but for the fact that he had a quick-witted helper.

It would seem that the whole village of Woodland

was gathered at the station to welcome back the young aeronauts from their mysterious journey.

Professor Kendrick, with fine tact, kept himself in the background.

It was the grandfather who stepped from the car and came forward leading the children, his worn face triumphant. Then the long repressed excitement of the multitude burst forth in a glad cheer and women wept and laughed by turns. They followed, a long procession, to the very door of the Reynolds' home, and many mothers could not be satisfied until they had taken the children into their arms and held them close.

Elizabeth Dorset was not obliged to depend, thereafter, upon the old astronomy for information concerning planets, for the professor was a whole mine of knowledge and an enthusiast besides. It came about that the Vailes and Dorsets made a party on the large porch almost every evening to gaze through the telescope. Two of the company often lingered after the others were wearied and gone. They had much to say to each other, and not altogether about heavenly bodies. These two had lived comparatively lonely lives heretofore; the professor, for the same reason that a woman often does, because he had never found his ideal, and Elizabeth had become skeptical whether ideals ever did crystallize into satisfactory human character as far as men were concerned—always accepting her father. The end of it all was that if those two should live a hundred years, and there should be a hundred comets, none could ever be so interesting to them as the one they were in search of that night they found each other.

KEEPING A FORGOTTEN TRYST

by

Grace Livingston Hill

(Originally published in 1901)

KEEPING A FORGOTTEN TRYST

Chapter 1

At Thirty-sixth Street a university student boarded the streetcar and took an empty seat in the front end. He wore the careless, self-satisfied look of many of the men of the younger classes, and he gazed about him with the indifference born of unconscious feeling of his own superiority over the other people in the car.

It was not an interesting carful to his mind. They were nearly all plain, weary-looking women. No pretty girls, and very few men. Opposite him sat a woman and a little boy about twelve years old. There was nothing especially noticeable about them, except that in some strange, intangible way the boy reminded him of himself at that age—bright black eyes, hair a-tumble under the cap, restless, eager movements—every bit a boy. A rather homely little fellow with a turned-up nose and a few freckles, but interesting because of the eagerness in his face.

And the mother—she was his mother, of course—
one would have known that without the clear voice
saying at the beginning of almost every sentence: "Say,
mother!" A shrinking little woman in gray who was
content to live unnoticed, she would not have been
looked at twice but for the eager interest with which she
seemed to enter into her boy's talk.

They discussed the trip downtown. It was evidently
a gala occasion, a trifle unusual. They planned in low
tones, which, nevertheless, in the boy's clear treble,
could be distinctly heard across the aisle, though it was
plain to be seen he was making an effort to keep the low
tones of refinement into which he had been trained, and
thought he was doing it.

"Mother, while you're looking at the bonnets I'll go
down in the basement for a while. There's a lot of things
I want to see, and especially the automobiles. I'll meet
you in the waiting-room in just half an hour, you know.
No, I won't get lost! Why, I know every inch of that store
like a book! Say, mother, that reminds me, Tom
Sandborn has the nicest book! He got it for his birthday.
We fellows had a lot of fun with it. It's all conundrums.
Say now, mother, hear this! If the alphabet were invited
out to supper, which of the letters would get there late?"

He looked up into her face, his eyes sparkling with
the answer, and his lips shutting tight over it, and she

looked down perplexedly at the toe of her shoe, as much in earnest over it as if she had been another boy. Several other people in the car were puzzling over the conundrum also, and one woman forgot to signal the conduct to stop till they had passed her street; but the two did not know. The mother looked up with an almost girlish uncertainty.

"Would it be 'l, a, t, and e'?" she asked, deprecatingly.

"No," said the boy, unable to keep the answer longer, "it would be all those letters which come after 't.'"

They enjoyed the witticism together in a subdued way, but the student across the aisle was struck by the friendship between mother and son. So his mother used to be with him. He watched them narrowly, almost enviously.

"And here's another, mother. See if you can get this: 'Why is a harsh schoolmaster like the eye?'"

"I'm sure I can't get that," said the mother, looking with admiring eyes into the bright, upturned face.

"Why, because he has a pupil ever under the lash!"

The student found himself smiling, and forgot his classic dignity. It seemed so like the dear years gone forever, when he had started out somewhere with his mother, and had told her all his boyish pleasures and repeated his new "finds" in fun and knowledge, mostly fun. And she had cared in just this way, and had looked down into his face with fondness and pride, just as this mother was doing with her happy boy.

If his mother, even now, had been at home toiling to keep her son in college, or if she had but been waiting for the years to turn around when he should come back to her a man, finished, and ready for a career in which she should live out her pride in him, he would doubtless not have been touched by this so tenderly. But his mother had been laid to rest from earth for seven years, and he had grown away from those far-off days when there was someone who loved him so. He had almost forgotten that he was ever childish enough to kiss his mother at night before he went to bed. Carefully packed away in the attic of his heart were the precepts she had taught him. He might use them sometime, but they were not the rules generally in use in the university. And he had grown to think that he had been but a child, and his mother—a woman. He was a *man* now. Almost lulled to sleep was the conscience she had so carefully trained. He could ride over it with a laugh now, and not feel a twinge of pain. By much abuse and the anesthetic of an atmosphere of unbelief, it was almost entirely benumbed.

But something in this simple mother-love and eager

boy roused his memory more than for many a year. He could hear that other boy telling of a birthday party some friend was to have. Ah, birthdays! How bright his own had been when his mother lived! He smiled to think how little had pleased him at twelve, and how his mother had taken pains to give him all those silly little things that go to make up the joy of the boy memory. How keen had been his delight over the gifts, and how swift his appreciation of the sacrifices his mother had undergone to secure some pleasures for him.

And her birthday had been as great a pleasure to him as his own. That last one! How well he remembered it. He had stayed away from school to enjoy it, and they had gone out in the country together, and studied wild flowers and had such a happy time, while she had told him stories of her girlhood days, with a hint of his father's wooing her, and a tear brushed hastily away at a tender memory of that dear father who had been taken from her and her boy so early.

The university student felt something choking in his throat, and turned to look out of the front window at his left. But the houses, telegraph poles, people, and wagons were a confused blur before him as his mind, once started, forced him through the memory of that day in every detail.

"And now, Ralph, we will go to prayer-meeting

together, and finish this beautiful day in the best of ways!" He could almost hear his mother's voice saying the words in his ear above the whir of the trolley, the clang of bell, and murmur of talk.

He could see his mother's sweet face as she sat in her accustomed place in prayer-meeting, and almost hear the tones of her voice, as she sang:

"I love thy kingdom, Lord!
 The house of thine above.
The church of blessed Redeemer saved
 With his own precious blood."

The very car wheels whirred the familiar old tune, and insisted on each word coming in in time. He could not get away from them if he chose, nor the vision of the old church with his mother by his side, singing. How she had loved the church!

"Isn't it nice, mother, that your birthday came on prayer-meeting night, so we could end the day by going together? It makes a beautiful evening, because you love the church so!" He could remember his own words on the way home from the meeting, and yet it all seemed ages ago. He could feel the pressure of her gentle hand on his arm in answer, and her sweet voice:

"Yes, dear. It would be nice if my birthdays always came on prayer-meeting nights, wouldn't it?"

And he had asked how long it would be before it again came on Wednesday, and had spent the rest of the walk in counting it up and allowing for leap years and announced to her triumphantly just how long it would be before her birthday fell on Wednesday, and they could finish the day with a prayer-meeting.

"I want you to promise me, Ralph, that when it comes, you will go to the prayer-meeting if you possibly can, no matter where you are."

And he, with his boyhood's readiness, had eagerly promised, with a bright: "With you, mother?" and she had smiled a little sadly, and said, as she stepped inside the door he had unlocked for her:

"Yes, dear, I can promise to go with you in spirit, if I am unable to be with you bodily."

That had been some time before she died. Was it two years? He could not remember distinctly. But that birthday prayer-meeting stood out clear before his mind—and his own promise. Strange he had not thought of it before!

Stay! Was not this the very year and month? Yes; and— What day was it? Wednesday! And the date? He took out a little pocket memorandum to make sure he was correct. Yes, it was this very night! How had he grown away from that dear mother, that the very date of her birthday, treasured so in years gone by, had slipped upon him unaware! Perhaps it would have gone by without his notice, and his promise remained forgotten if it had not been for the bright-faced boy and his mother opposite.

He glanced at them again. The boy was detailing to his mother all he had done and said, and all that the other boys had said the day before at a friend's house. Just as he used to do. But could he do it now? Would his daily pursuits and companions' conversation always bear the test of those clear, dear mother-eyes? He turned away from the two opposite with annoyance in his face.

It suddenly came over him that he was pledged to attend quite a different assembly that evening from the church prayer-meeting his mother had chosen. What would his mother think of tonight's escapade?

Not that there was anything very dreadful in the plan, either. Just a few of the fellows were going on a lark in an automobile with a few girls, to take supper several miles in the country at a hotel, and return by moonlight. True, the girls were merry, and the men were fun-loving, but there was nothing really bad about them. Up to this minute it had not seemed to him to be going out of the path of right. But now, in the light of his mother's face, he suddenly saw things differently.

What would his mother think of the boys and their jokes? Would she choose the kind of girls for his

companions who were to go with them that night? What
of the money all this would cost? Would she think he
had a right to spend so much from his meager
allowance, which must carry him through his education
and fit him for life? His conscience had suffered twinges
on this account before. But then he had gone into it
before he had realized how much it was to cost, and
there was no backing out now. He would be called mean.
He must pay his share, for he had promised.

Ah! But he had promised his mother years before!
Even though he had been but a child his heart
recognized the bindingness of the first promise. It
chilled him to think he could not keep tryst with that
loving mother.

Somehow the years were strangely bridged over all
at once. He drew his hand in perplexity across his brow.
He must not break his promise to the dead! But how
could he help it?

There was a sudden vision of the stylish girl who
was to be his companion that evening. She was a
handsome girl, with a cloud of fluffy black hair in a very
decided pompadour over her face, and eyes that could
scintillate. She was a great favorite among the boys. She
knew how to be witty on occasion, and was not over
particular about chaperones. It was a special honor that
she had allowed him to take her tonight, and until a few

minutes before he had felt quite elated; but now the memory of her rather loud voice and free manners grated on him as he thought of his gentle mother standing by and listening with grieved eyes to see how her dear boy had changed!

Of a sudden he knew that he could not go on the frolic that night. He must keep the tryst with his mother. He shut his lips tight with resolve. He would go and see Josephine at once. It would be a tough job, and she would have nothing more to do with him, of course, but perhaps that was just as well. He would hate it and the boys would guy him a lot. But a long-forgotten strength came to him. His mother stood beside him. Almost he could feel her hand upon his arm, and a thrill of longing to bring a smile to her face passed over him. He would not disappoint her even though she was dead.

The car had stopped and the mother and boy were going out. The boy swung himself easily out before her and took her hand to help her down, and the student looked with jealous eyes. If he could but have his mother for one short afternoon!

With a quick motion he jumped to his feet and went to the platform, where he swung himself off the moving car with the ease of an athlete and went down a side street. Without pausing to reflect he rushed in at a great stone doorway and took the elevator to the sixth floor.

He scarcely waited for the grating door to open wide before he was out and hastening down the marble hall to an office door. Several men were at desks, and two young women at typewriters were rapidly clicking away. He paused by the door and asked if he might see Miss Carter. Then he saw Josephine coming toward him, smiling, and a little surprised at his sudden advent, and it occurred to him that he did not know what he was going to say to her.

Chapter 2

There was something in Miss Carter's air as she moved
slowly toward him from her desk by a pleasant window,
passing the two typewriter girls without even seeming
to see them, that made the young man remember her
position in this office. He had not a very distinct idea
what it was, and he became conscious that he had once
been told something about how much she was valued
and what a bright young woman she was. Whether she
was at the head of some department, or was merely a
bookkeeper or confidential clerk he was not sure, but
certain it was that a deference was paid to her here
which was not accorded to the two typewriter girls.

She swept by the men in the office like a queen, and
the visitor suddenly felt that he would rather be
anywhere else than here on such an errand. It had not
seemed, out in the street, that he had so very dreadful a
task before him, but face to face with Josephine Carter
it was a different thing. Also, there was a slight lifting of

126

her eyebrows that indicated that it must be a weighty matter which had made him dare intrude upon her during business hours unbidden.

She paused before him, her greeting touched with the question of why he had come. And then he hunted around for a single instant for some excuse to get away. He might say he merely called to know if she was informed as to the hour of starting, or if she were well, or—

Bah! She would think him a fool! She was too keen not to see through anything like that. Had he not talked it over most carefully with her but the night before? And nothing had been changed. There was not the slightest possible thing he could think of that he had not already told her about the arrangements—nothing but the truth! And then he looked up into her great dark eyes, and saw beside them the sweet blue ones of his mother looking at him so trustingly. This steadied him. As a little boy the sight or the thought of his mother had ever had the power to steady nerves and give courage. His embarrassment was gone in a minute, and with that almost haughty toss of his head that had made Miss Carter admire him enough to allow herself to be his companion for the evening he spoke:

"I have called, Miss Carter, to ask you to excuse me this evening from the ride to which I invited you. I know it is a rude thing to do, and I feel awfully cut up about it, but I really cannot go."

"You cannot go?" repeated the young woman, growing decidedly haughty herself. "I do not understand. What has happened? Is the party broken up? Has there been a falling out?"

His face grew red. It was harder than he had thought. The dark eyes were scrutinizing him coldly, and he lost sight of the blue ones for the moment.

"No, the party is going, and there has been no trouble anywhere so far as I know, only with myself. I find I cannot go."

"Do you mean that someone else, then, is to take me?" Miss Carter drew herself up with a manner that was not to be trifled with.

"No, why—I—" Then eagerly, "Why, yes, I could arrange something like that if you are willing."

"Oh, then I *am* to be consulted about the matter!" she said. "I did not know but it was all arranged. Most certainly you need not be put to that trouble! But why, may I ask, are you not able to keep your appointment and take me yourself?"

Her voice was quiet and controlled, but he could see by the rising flush on her face that she was angry. It was a trying position for her. He had not looked at it much from her standpoint before. Perhaps he ought not to have done this after all. He wished with all his heart he were back in the trolley, and had never seen or heard of that woman and her child. The idea of such a thing upsetting all his plans! And then he looked up with growing embarrassment to try to explain and again the calm blue eyes smiled at him.

"I have to go somewhere else," he replied.

"And why did you not know this last evening?" asked the young woman, cuttingly.

"I had forgotten it," he said with lowered eyes and an almost shame in his voice, and he felt that he was making the confession to his mother; not only of the promise for the evening but of all the teachings he had forgotten since she went away.

Josephine Carter was angry and disappointed. Moreover there was not a little pique mingled with her feelings. She was very anxious for an automobile ride, and such expensive luxuries did not often come her way. Besides she had taken a decided liking to the student, who, though a trifle younger than herself, was bright and good company. She had been anticipating an enjoyable flirtation during the evening. It was altogether a new experience to have a *young* student treat her condescension in this way. She was a favorite, and knew it. She did not intend to be treated so if she could help it. Yet in spite of her anger she could see behind the young man's manner that there was something unusual the matter. She was enough a woman of the world to be a pretty good reader of human nature, and she was interested and curious.

"Is it another engagement?" she asked, after looking him over for a moment. Her voice had softened somewhat. Perhaps he was getting into mischief somewhere and she could save him. That would be interesting. She would use her arts of persuasion, which never failed in an emergency. With her most winning smile she looked upon him.

"Break it!" she said suddenly. "Break it for me! I want to go on that ride dreadfully. It is going to be fine, and I set my heart upon it!"

"I cannot," he said. "It was made long ago," and he raised his face, white now, to the other eyes that looked at him behind hers.

She felt that she had not his full attention. She bit her lips with vexation. He did not even *see* how she was stooping to him. She frowned and tapped her foot impatiently.

"It is something you are ashamed of," she charged at hazard.

The color flamed into his face, but he answered only, "No!"

A sudden daring came into her eyes. "Then take me

with you!" she retorted.

Now, indeed, his embarrassment arose a new.

"You—would not care to go," he answered hesitatingly. He could not tell her where he was going. She would laugh. She would make him the butt of all the college jokes. He would never hear the last of it. In what a position had he allowed himself to be placed that he could not go to a prayer-meeting without it seeming an extraordinary thing! How he had fallen since the days when he and mother used to go, and love it! Would his mother know him now if she could come back again?

"Oh, certainly, I should be delighted to go. It must be a very choice entertainment that has power to take you from the ride tonight, and upset the whole arrangement generally. May I inquire if the rest of the party know of your extraordinary change of mind?" There was mockery in her tone.

His own anger was rising. It was miserable to be tortured in this way. He had a right to do as he pleased.

"No, I have not told them. I came first to ask you to release me from my engagement with you. I am sorry that it causes you disappointment, and wish that I could undo this horrible bungle I have made; but so far as the party is concerned, it will make no possible difference to them. I shall, of course, pay what I have agreed to pay toward the affair, and they will have more room. I beg your pardon. I should have remembered that it will make a great difference to some of the party not to have you with them, but as you were to have been my guest I suppose that I should be the main loser in that way. I beg, Miss Carter, that you will release me."

There was a stubbornness and a rising hauteur about him now that made the young lady determined not to be defeated.

"Most certainly, Mr. Baldwin, I shall *not* release you. You have engaged my company for the evening, and I shall accompany you. If not on the ride, then to the other destination, wherever it may be that compels you to change your plans."

She was half-frightened at what she had done after she said the words, and she studied his face narrowly through half-shut lashes.

He looked up to see if she really meant it.

"As you please," he said curtly. "I will call for you at half-past seven," and lifting his hat was gone.

"Mr. Baldwin!" she called a little breathlessly just as he reached the elevator. She must have moved rapidly indeed to be standing beside him so soon. He had come with strides as long as those that brought him to her a few minutes before.

"Aren't you going to tell me where you are going to take me?" she questioned, almost timidly.

"Oh, that is not necessary," he said. "If you insist upon going you can certainly trust me to take you to a respectable place. Good afternoon."

The elevator door slammed shut with a click and the car had vanished from the floor, leaving her standing bewildered by the empty shaft.

Downstairs a perplexed and angry young man was striding toward the Walnut Street trolley-car, unable to settle clearly in his mind for which of the several disagreeable positions in which he had been successively placed he was the most to blame.

Chapter 3

Josephine Carter did not render the firm that employed her the usual valuable assistance during the remainder of that afternoon. She was a girl who enjoyed a spice of daring and adventure, but there was something about this affair that rather frightened her. A dozen times that afternoon she told herself that Mr. Baldwin would not come for her at all—as many times declared she would not go with him unless he told her all. And yet, down deep in her heart she knew that she would. Her curiosity was aroused, and she did not intend to be beaten by a mere "boy," she told herself.

As the afternoon waned, the question of dress came up. What in the world should she wear? How could she know where he would take her, and what would be appropriate? She rather prided herself on dressing well. It would not do to go in full dress, and make herself conspicuous, neither would she like to be behind others if full-dress was the thing. But, as there was no possible way of telling until it was too late to change her costume, she must strike a happy medium in a gown that would not be conspicuous either way. She must be ready if she would carry out her purpose. It would not do to keep him waiting if he were in the same state of mind as that afternoon; she could see that. She wisely resolved to be ready.

Meantime, she resolutely refused to listen to the palpitating of her heart, or the voice that told her she should be careful where she was going; that she did not know this young man. She shut her lips firmly, and told her conscience that she knew how to take care of herself. She would keep her eyes open. Nevertheless, she awaited his coming in the parlor of her boarding house with no little trepidation.

Ralph Baldwin, meanwhile, was seated in another trolley-car glaring at the people across from him without even seeing them. He ground his teeth over his discomfort. A more miserable ride he never took. He wished himself many times far away. He wished he had not come to college; had never seen the fellows who had led him into reckless ways; had never seen the boy and his mother who had made a soft-hearted fool of him that afternoon; had never made a promise which was so much trouble to keep; had never remembered it till it was too late to keep it; had never heard of automobiles, nor planned to take a ride in one.

Above all, he wished he had never seen or heard of Miss Josephine Carter. Her pretty face below the softly waving pompadour that, but a few hours before, had seemed so charming, now grew detestable. She mocked him from every car window out of which he looked. How she would mock tonight! There was no use getting out of it. He was in for a regular time of it in some way. Should he bluff it off by taking her to the theater? No; his mother's eyes would haunt him. He must keep that promise now he had remembered it. Besides, she would know he had not carried out his purpose. He would never have given up the ride for the theater. It was as well. It would serve her right. He judged correctly that she would not select a prayer-meeting as a place of amusement. If she would go she would be well punished. He devoutly hoped that she would repent before evening, and declined to go unless he told her all—and that he would not do. It showed what kind of girl she was to go to an unknown place with a comparative stranger. His fancy, or whatever it was that had been attracted by her, was no longer blinded. He was done with such a girl. Nevertheless, he would be honorable, and keep his appointment with her, much as he longed to sneak out of it by not calling for her at all.

There was another question that worried him as he

drew near the university. He must tell the other fellows something. He studied his toes, and tried to think of some way of putting things that would not bring an onslaught of wrath upon his head. At last he decided to wait until the last minute, and send word he could not go. This would, at least, delay the storm of questions that was sure to come until the morrow. Perhaps something would turn up by that time to help him out.

He reached his room without meeting any of the party who were to go on the ride that evening. He had almost expected to see them waiting to waylay him, and shouting at him from every corner. He closed and locked his door, and reflected that it would be as well to keep it locked for a while if he wished to escape meeting any of the fellows. He settled himself to his much neglected studies. From the pages his mother's eyes looked out reproachfully. Could it be that she knew how he had been wasting his time in college? She who had always been so proud of his ability to learn quickly, and had told him he had his father's bright mind?

He tried to bring himself to study. He suddenly realized that he must meet this book in a recitation tomorrow, for which he was not prepared. The memory of other recitations met and passed in the same way brought a realization that his standing in college was being sorely imperiled. He must make a change, must not let his chance of an education, with his young life and his little money, slip from him this way, and leave him penniless and ignorant to begin the fight with the world.

The words in the book he held before his eyes were written in Greek, but they might have been written in Arabic, or some other unknown tongue, for the language of the lesson he studied that afternoon was the language of the soul.

Twice there came steps to his door, and several peremptory knocks followed; but he remained motionless, with his eyes on the book. It was no part of his plan to be heard or seen just now. A hand tried his door the last time, and he heard an exclamation of impatience; then the steps went away, and all was still again.

Out of his window he could hear, during the temporary quiet of the humming street, the clatter of supper dishes in a boarding house not far away, and a whiff of something fried floated up to him. But he was not hungry. He hated the thought of going to supper.

By and by he reached for his pen, and wrote a hasty note, addressed to the chief mover in the evening affair, telling him he had suddenly found he could not come, but that he would pay his part, and they must not wait for him. He had arranged it with the young lady. He set his lips grimly as he wrote the last sentence and signed his name. How he had arranged matters with the young lady he was yet to see.

He glanced at his watch, and hailed a messenger boy from the window. The note was sent on its way, and he hastily made his toilet for prayer-meeting, and slipped out an unaccustomed door to the back street. If anyone came to look him up they would have hard work to find him.

He had studied so long over that Greek book that 7:30 was rapidly drawing near. He looked anxiously at his watch as he boarded the car which would take him to Miss Carter's boarding place. He found himself building great hopes that she would not go, after all. The strain would be something terrible. How could he bear to have her by his side as he kept the tryst with his dear mother? A tenderness and a deep yearning for his mother had come over him during that hour he had spent alone. The fountain of memory once unsealed, many events that he had not thought of for years had moved in procession before him. Miss Carter he counted as a interruption and in incongruity with his new thoughts. And, worst of all, how could he tell her he was going to *prayer-meeting?*

His face was set and stern as he mounted the white marble steps and rang the bell. His heart sank within him as he saw, on reaching the parlor, his lady in hat, coat, and gloves, fully ready. So, then, she was determined! He shut his lips tightly. Very well! She should have no satisfaction from him. Let her find it out as she would.

She met him with gay, bantering speech. It was the only way she knew to carry off her position gracefully. But he gravely looked at his watch and said:

"It is well you are entirely ready, as it is growing late."

The car that went downtown was almost at the door. He took two steps ahead to signal it to stop, and helped her in. There was no time for talk. And, once inside the car, they were separated, she taking a seat near the front, which a gentleman rose to give her, and he standing on the platform, for the car was crowded. He was thankful for this. He could not bear the thought of talking to her.

And there, in the solitude of the crowded platform, he abruptly realized that he did not know himself know where he was taking her. He had put her on board this car instinctively, knowing that it went downtown, and that he wished to get away from the vicinity of the university, and all who knew him. But where was a prayer-meeting to be found? In some church, of course; and it mattered little what church, so long as it was a prayer-meeting, and he carried out his promise and got himself through with this miserable business. But, of course, he must decide where.

He was somewhat of a stranger in the city as regarded churches. He might, of course, walk till he came to a church. One would not be far to find in such a large Christian city is this; but that would not do when he had Miss Carter for a companion. He must know decidedly what he was going to do before he got off that car.

He looked at the well-groomed crowd about him, and longed to have their knowledge of churches for a moment, but would rather have cut out his tongue then ask. He must think hard and fast. Where had he heard of a minister downtown? Ah! What was the name of that famous teacher of whom he had heard so often? He was quite an orator, and crowds went to his church, insomuch that they were forced to issue tickets to the Sunday services. He had always intended going to hear him sometime, there had been so much said about him. Would such a church have a prayer-meeting? Probably, for he had heard that one of the fads of this preacher was to have the church open all the time. Yes, there would be something going on. And, fortunately, he knew the whereabouts of that church tolerably well.

A word with the conductor told him where to

change to the cross trolley, and he stood up and looked about him breathing freely again. How could he have been so careless as to have left that question of the church undecided before he started out? The perspiration stood out on his forehead as he reflected what his companions would say, could they ever know of it.

The car stopped at the usual haunts of the theatergoers, and the crowds poured out. Miss Carter watched her escort anxiously for a signal, but he seemed not to see her. The seats beside her were still filled. She was relieved at last when a little further downtown he motioned her to get out. She had a storm of questions ready to pour at him when they reached the sidewalk, for her ride had been an anxious one, as well as his, but again opportunity was not favorable. The car which she saw by his attitude that they were to take was almost upon them, and it, too, was well filled with people standing. She hastily selected the question she most wished answered, and asked it in a queer choking voice not quite like her own:

"Mr. Baldwin, is this engagement—with—another—another lady?"

He looked at her grimly after a moment's hesitation and answered, "It is," and then she was obliged to step on the car and again be seated at the other end from where he stood.

They were in a part of the town she did not know so well now, and the people in the car were most of them going home from work of one sort and another. They were not on their way to the theater. She studied the numbers anxiously as they whirred by block after block, and tried to remember all that she had ever heard about this part of the town. When they left the car at last they had but a few steps to walk, and she was unable to summon her courage, or to decide what words to speak to break the silence.

A massive stone building rose before them. She could not tell from the dusk, mingled with gaslight, what sort of the building it was. An arched doorway was in front of them, letting out a flood of brightness upon the pavement; and people were going in. There was a sound of singing; the words and tone were unfamiliar, but reassuring. She glanced at her companion curiously and followed where he led.

Chapter 4

A young usher met them at the inner door and led them to chairs, while another, a freshman in the university, whom the young men knew slightly, smiled and handed them a hymn-book open to the hymn that was being sung.

Perhaps if Ralph Baldwin had searched through the whole of that staid city he could not have found another such prayer-meeting. If some magic telescope could but have given glimpses into many dimly-lighted prayer-rooms where a few saints were gathered, singing—

"The church has waited long
Her absent Lord to see,"

—with a feeling that she would still continue to wait comfortably many thousand years to come, it would have been a decided contrast to the warm, enthusiastic meeting in which they now found themselves.

But Ralph Baldwin did not realize this. He had

144

unconsciously expected to enter a quiet, sacred spot like the old chapel at home where he and his mother used to go, with the very air was hushed in solemn expectation as the people tip-toed in and bowed their heads. The singing would be slow and wavering, but would come deep from the hearts of the worshipers because they were singing "unto the Lord." There would be a few good old elders who would pray a long time, and he should feel again, perhaps, the same reverent thrill of unspeakable awe that he used to feel as a little boy when he tried to realize that these venerable men were speaking to God, and He, the Creator of the universe, was in that room, listening. He remembered once picking up half-frightened at the long white beard, and closed eyes shaded by shaggy eyebrows, of one such good old man, and wondering how he came to be so very good, and to dare to talk to God before others.

He had hoped to feel his mother's presence by his side all that evening. She had promised to be with him in spirit, and his longing heart wondered if she could come.

But here all was different. The room was a blaze of electric light. The singing was joyous. "It is good to be here, it is good to be here," they were singing, and the faces about looked as if they meant it. And there were no empty seats. Every chair was filled. A few even were sitting on some wooden stools about the platform. It looked more like a big family gathering of good cheer and hearty praise than the formal prayer-meeting of today or the quiet, solemn ones of former times. Not that it was any nearer to the Master than the sacred gatherings of the few, wherein he always meets, or better calculated to keep mortal souls in touch with their Maker. The old times and ways were good, but so were the new ones, and they sometimes fit the new circumstances a little better than the old.

The prayers that followed the singing in this meeting were brief and to the point, made by men who had not attained great things as yet, most of them; poor, humble, seeking, striving ones, who could boast no long lives of service, but who were newly enlisted and scarce accustomed yet to speaking familiarly with their new Master. But they one and all voiced their petitions with a ring of true earnestness and a simple trust in this new-found Friend of theirs.

At another time this young student, who had been at the University only long enough to think he knew it all, and had not yet learned how much he had to learn, might have smiled or sneered at the formation of some of the sentences, but another spirit was within him tonight, and he scarcely noticed any slips of grammar in a few of the illiterate who spoke. He scarcely knew which was learned and which ignorant, but felt the spell of the brotherly love that here bound all classes together. They were all children of one Father whom they loved. He used to feel that he belonged, too. How good it would be to have his boyish trust once more unshaken, and to kneel beside his bed tonight—sure, sure that God was leading him in all his ways and would take care of him all his days. He drew a deep sigh, and the girl by his side, of whom he had become entirely oblivious, looked at him curiously. She had given the problem up entirely. In vain had she searched the faces of the audience for some pretty girl who had been the attraction to this meeting. Her escort neither spoke nor looked at anyone save the young usher. He seemed to be as much a stranger as she.

Meetings full of life and earnestness were more familiar to her than to him perhaps. She had been accustomed to lively gatherings in the country church at home before she left her old father and mother and brothers and sisters on the farm, and came to the city to make a place for herself in the world more to her liking. And she had not deserted her old habits all at once either, only dropped them little by little. Even now when she had nothing better to do she strayed into some church on a Sunday, but she was used enough to it that it did not seem strange to her. She thought at first that perhaps he had brought her here for fun, and that he would presently make her understand. But his grave face gave no sign.

One unusual thing about this prayer-meeting was that the pastor sat at a little organ on the platform and played for the singing himself, mostly without notes, leading the audience in a rich, full tenor voice. There was no show about any of it. Everything was sung as a part of the worship, and came from the heart.

During a slight pause following a prayer a man stepped up to the pastor and whispered a few words, to which he bowed assent.

"My brother asks for 'My Mother's Prayer' to be sung," he said in explanation, and a soft stir of pleasure moved over the people as they settled to listen. Then the pastor touched a few chords and with closed eyes sang, speaking distinctly the words of a quaint descriptive song of the old home and its memories; of the trundle bed, the time of prayer, and the mother's lullaby and nightly benediction.

It was a gospel song, touching and tender. There was nothing wonderful about the music, and the words were homely, but this audience liked it. It brought back tender memories to their hearts, and the face of the man who had requested the singing was wet with tears. He had a mother who prayed thus beside him. Some might

laugh at such a song in a prayer-meeting, so odd and
queer and unconventional, but this audience was quiet
and devout as the singing went on.

But there was one soul in the room who had not
caught the spirit. To Miss Carter the song was
inimitably funny, and that the minister should sing it
made it all the more irresistible. Now indeed had the
"show" she had been waiting for begun. There was
doubtless more to follow, and her escort had known
what he was about when he brought her. Her mouth
stretched wide in a broad laugh, which showed all her
little white teeth, it was considered quite bewitching in
her. She turned to her companion with instant readiness
to forgive his past offenses, and enjoy with him this
performance. She even made a slight motion, and
cleared her throat to show him she understood; but to
her astonishment his face was graver than ever as he
looked earnestly at the singer, and seemed to be really
listening intently.

"While I listen to that music
  Stealing on in gentle strain,
I am carried back to childhood—
  I am now a child again;
'Tis the hour of my retiring,
  At the dusky eventide;
Near my trundle-bed I'm kneeling
  As of yore by mother's side.

"Hands are on my head so loving
　As they were in childhood's days;
I, with weary tones, am trying
　To repeat the words she says;
'Tis a prayer in language simple
　As a mother's lips can frame;
'Father, thou who are in heaven
　Hallowed ever be thy name.'

"Then my mother, o'er me bending,
　Prays in earnest words, but mild:
'Hear my prayer, O heavenly father,
　Bless, O bless my precious child.'

"Yet I am but only dreaming;
　Ne'er I'll be a child again;
Many years has that dear mother
　In the quiet churchyard lain;
But the mem'ry of her counsels
　O'er my path a light has shed,
Daily calling me to heaven
　Even from my trundle-bed."

She had watched him closely during the singing. Gradually the tenderness of the words crept into her consciousness. As the last verse was being sung her curious eyes saw a tear trembling in his, and before the end was reach he had put up his hand hastily, and covered his face.

It was only for an instant, and then he was himself again, but she dropped her gaze in confusion, and hoped he had not known she was watching him.

During the remainder of that meeting she sat is quiet grave as he did. She had looked, unawares, into the open door of a room where a soul lived—and where others were not meant to look—but in that instant she had seen in that room a mirror which had reflected her own soul, and it was with herself she had to do the rest of that evening

What was the subject of that meeting, or what the pastor's earnest little talk near the close, those two, perhaps, will never know. It simply emphasized to them the impressions they had gained from earlier life and made them think of home and mother and her teaching as they had not thought for years.

They went silently out with the crowd, and walked to the corner where they would have to take the car before either spoke.

"Will you tell me please," said Miss Carter, in a subdued voice, "who is the woman that made you promise to go there tonight? Was she there?"

He looked at her gravely for a moment and then in a new tone of decision and self-respect he answered:

"It was my mother. And—yes—I think she was there!"

They had to get into the car then, but by and by Miss Carter summoned courage to question him again, and he told her in a few words of his promise, adding:

"My mother has been in heaven seven years, and I have forgotten sometimes, but I think she was there tonight, for *she* always kept her promises."

The theatergoers were pouring into the other cars when they changed, and there was little opportunity for talk, but as they were once more going up the steps of her boardinghouse she put out her hand impulsively and touched his arm.

"Forgive me, will you?" She said. "I only meant to have some fun. I'm sorry I have made it hard for you. I have a mother, too, and she isn't in heaven, either, I'm thankful to say, though I have not remembered her always."

There was the sound of a sob in her voice as she said the last words, and he grasped her hand warmly and said good night in a tone that she felt meant he would forgive.

That night, in her room, after long, earnest thinking she got out her mother's last letter, read it over, cried over it, and then sat up very late to write a long answer, such as would delight the hearts that should read it.

And at the university, in his room, there knelt beside his bed a young man seeking his mother's God, and going over the past few years with repentance; while above the angels keeping watch want with swift wings to tell the story of the return of the prodigal.

YOU and I

by

Marcia Livingston

(Originally published in 1893)

YOU and I

Margaret Wayland, though not a beauty in any strict sense of the term, was a fair sight to look upon as she walked down the leaf-strewn street that October afternoon. Her white flannel gown with a scarlet maple leaf or two tucked in the belt was just the sort of dress which best suited her. Margaret was peculiar as to looks; much depended on her setting and her moods. She might wear the robe of a princess for richness and not be at her best if the tint did not harmonize with the blue gray of the wearer's eyes, nor bring out the delicate color in her face. One seeing her as she looked that afternoon—a soft flush on her cheeks, dark eyes glowing, joyful energy in every line and curve, and the sunshine turning her brown hair to reddish gold—would have pronounced her beautiful. But the next day when Margaret donned a dark dress of unbecoming color and her rather pale face was in shadow, especially if the calm of her spirit had been ruffled by any of the small squalls which overtake the best of us—for she was not perfect, this girl—why, then one might reconsider the verdict of yesterday.

Ruskin's recipe for making a girl beautiful is happiness. As a rule, the light of content shown in Margaret's eyes, and the curves of her mouth were sweet, which could not be, of course, unless she were sweet-spirited; so on the whole, she must have been beautiful, let critics say what they will.

It was an ideal life, as far as moderate means can make it so, that Margaret lived with her grandparents. Since she came to them a two-year-old baby, bereft of father and mother, they had seemed to exist but for her sake. She might have grown up a "pink and white tyrant" but that prompt obedience was exacted of her though the discipline had been mild and loving in the extreme.

It was pleasant to watch the girl as she skipped over the walk to the old-fashioned stone house, up the white steps through the door into the hall, where, taking off her hat, she went on into the dining room, tied on ample blue checked apron and busied herself in preparations for the evening meal. There was an unskilled girl in the kitchen for heavy work, but the fine arts of housekeeping devolved upon Margaret. Those who insist the grace in a woman is inconsistent with swift movement should have watched her as she flitted about, carefully taking down quaint, delicate china, precious heirlooms, toasting thin slices of bread to just the right shade of brown and brewing the tea in the queer little teapot, with just that exquisite flavor which nice taste demands.

Then as they sat at supper it was a picture—the cozy, low-ceilinged room, the wide fireplace, a pine knot blazing, and easy chairs either side; the table laid with pretty care, a bowl of bright asters in the center; the stately grandfather, silver haired, the sweet-faced grandmother dressed in gray, adorned with soft, white hair and white kerchief, and the sparkling face of the girl as she rehearsed to them the fun and frolic of the day spent in the woods with a merry company, for grandpa and grandma were confidential friends, sharers of all her joys. In her they lived the past over again, happy in her pleasures, intensely sympathetic in her pains. Why, if Margaret had a headache Grandma Wayland found herself walking softly lest she should jar her own head, half thinking it was herself who bore the pain.

Into such a home came a cruel change. Mr. Wayland was not rich, but in that state of neither poverty nor riches, which promises best for quiet content. He had his little fortune as he supposed wisely invested, and with economy there was ample to maintain them in comfort and give to Margaret such advantages as could be found in a private school in the suburb where they lived, though to this was added a course of reading with her grandfather, a man of intellectual ability and fine taste which gave her a certain culture unusual in a girl of her years.

It was in the midst of the financial storm of that year that Mr. Wayland lost his property. At first it was only the failure of one or two investments, but other disasters followed in quick succession. The day before Christmas, as he and his wife sat together, the fateful letter was handed him with news that the bank where he had a large deposit had gone down, and in consequence of this a man who held a note endorsed by Mr. Wayland had also failed! And he? He was absolutely penniless.

Suppressing the exclamation of distress which rose to his lips at the first glance, he read it again, over and over, half-hoping he had mistaken its meaning. But there it was in black and white, the hard facts. This bank to break that he had thought firm as the old hills! He groaned inwardly as he recalled that he had withdrawn investments from other places and deposited them there because it was the very safest place. Had it not stood, unwavering, hundred years or more—his own forefathers its officers? There was not even the hope held out that a fragment might be saved to him.

Everything would be swept away, even the home that sheltered them.

His first thought was to keep it from his wife until after Christmas. But when he looked up, her eyes were resting on him. She had been watching the workings of his pale, troubled face, and wise woman that she was, had waited in silence, knowing that sooner or later he would come with his troubles to her. He handed the letter over to her now with a wan smile, saying:

"I would have kept it from you till after Christmas, dear, but I see by your looks you know that something is wrong. I may as well come out with it."

He leaned his head on his hand, and shaded his eyes, occasionally glancing at his wife apprehensively, wondering if the shock would be more than she could bear. Presently he saw her eyes close, and a look come into her face which meant she was sending a swift silent petition for help to the Great Helper.

She folded the letter calmly, and, drawing her chair nearer, slipped her hand into her husband's without speaking. He held it in a strong clasp, straightening himself and lifting his head almost proudly, as if to challenge any earthly circumstances to cloud his faith and hope, repeating in firm tones:

"Though he slay me, yet will I trust him. Eh, Elizabeth?"

And she answered softly, "Yes, Nathaniel, always."

Well might the heart of her husband safely trust in this woman, because of her perfect trust in him. It never crossed her mind to hint to him that he should have foreseen the failure, or that he ought not to sign the note.

When he began to recast his judgment, as people will in extremities and say, "I don't know, perhaps I ought not to have signed the note," she said to him:

"Don't, Nathaniel. Did you think at the time you were doing the wise, right thing?"

"Yes, I did. It seemed entirely safe, and I was under obligations to Burnham. He was very kind to me once."

"Then don't think any more about it. It's all right, somehow."

The next thing these two brave old souls set themselves to do was hide the ill news from Margaret until after Christmas. Almost the first thought her grandmother had, after reading the letter, was of thankfulness that the dear child's gifts were already bought, and the turkey, with its accessories, safe in the pantry; the day might not be clouded for her.

So the preparations for the simple festivities went on as usual in the old house. Margaret's glad Christmas carol trilled out, and, as usual, they were to share their dinner with some who had no good cheer of their own.

The poor widow across the way, with her two children, was invited, and, because of this, another Guest was present at their table that day and left His blessing.

It was easier to resolve to keep the ill news from Margaret than to do it. She was one of those sensitive natures who detect the slightest change in any atmosphere, physical or spiritual; and, though the words of her grandparents were cheerful, and their faces calm on Christmas morning, she detected a certain something in their bearing that was unusual; perhaps it was an added tenderness toward herself.

"What is the matter with you and grandpa today?" she asked. "You look as if you knew something that you haven't told me, or as if I were going off to leave you. I am not. You don't think of running away from me, do you? Don't look so sweet and solemn, grandma; it makes my heart ache."

The grandmother only answered with a smile. "It's time to set the table, now dear. Make it pretty. There are some chrysanthemums, you know." But to her own heart she said, with a sigh:

"Oh, who can tell what is to be? The dear child leave us! Will it come to that?" And then she resolutely put it out of her mind and went and brought crumbs to throw to the snowbirds, calling Margaret to see how much they enjoyed their Christmas dinner. Though while she watched them the thought would come to her, suggested by Satan, doubtless:

"Ah! You will be as badly off as the birds soon. You will not even have crumbs to throw away in the years to come. You're going to be poor now. Poor, poor!"

Even the snowbirds, as they ate and chirped, seemed to say: "Poor! Poor! Poor!" It was made to ring in her ears with satanic maliciousness. But, curiously now, there came to her mind a forgotten, quaint old hymn of her childhood. She repeated a verse of it to Margaret:

"Lord, according to thy words,
   I have considered thy birds;
And I find their life good,
   And better the better understood;
Sowing neither corn nor wheat;
   They have all that they can eat;
Reaping no more than they sow,
   They have all they can stow;
Having neither barn nor store;
   Hungry again, they eat more.
It cometh, therefore, to this, Lord:
   I have considered thy word,
And henceforth, will be thy bird."

The words cheered her fainting spirit, and Satan was baffled for that time.

Mr. Wayland, having earned rest by a laborious life, had, during these last years, taken his ease, devoting himself mainly to his books and the care of his garden and fruit trees. It was hard to bestir himself in his old age, and seek means for earning daily bread for his family.

He had been a prosperous druggist, and now sought clerkship in that trade, but experience availed nothing; he was old, and scores of young men stood ready for all vacant positions.

"My old horse was turned into a good pasture when he got too old for work," he told his wife with grim humor one night, "but an old man—he is a miserable animal, kicked out, good for nothing."

"Nathaniel," exclaimed his wife, pitying reproof in eye and voice—then added an apology for him: "You are very tired, dear."

As the house need not be vacated until spring, Mrs. Wayland added to their little store of ready money by taking a few borders, teachers in the seminary. Margaret was still in ignorance of their changed circumstances, and wondered not a little that her grandmother so burdened herself. It had been decided not to tell her for the present, but let her go on with her studies undisturbed, as she would be the better fitted for earning a livelihood.

When winter melted into spring and nothing had yet opened for Mr. Wayland, it would seem that the strongest faith would waiver. Meantime, all the worry and exposure worked mischief. He fell ill of rheumatism; not the comfortable kind—if there be a comfortable fiend of that name—consisting of a few occasional twinges, or slight lameness, necessitating an easy chair and ministrations of friends. This was the racking, tearing pain which threatened to sever body and soul, and called for all manly fortitude and patience, of which any man has but a small stock for such commonplace pains as rheumatism or neuralgia, yet the same grumbling individual would probably, with courage sublime, march unflinchingly to the stake, and be burned up once for all, if conscience so required.

To the rescue in these dark days came now Mrs. Sinclair, who had been a friend of Margaret's mother. She was at the head of a woman's college, and offered the daughter of her dearest friend a three year's course with a home in her family meantime, thus to be perfectly fitted for teaching. As the offer was gladly accepted, she advised that Margaret return at once with her and spend the summer in making ready to enter a certain class of the school for the fall term. This sudden parting was heartbreaking to all three. It was the bitterest drop in the bitter-cup.

When the morning came for their departure Mrs. Sinclair went early to the station that she might attend to checks and tickets, leaving Margaret to say her good-byes and follow at her leisure.

It was strange that there should come an added sting to the girl's sorrow at this time.

Just as she was passing through the gate "for the very last time," she told herself, a young man on horseback halted in front of it, lifted his hat, and, bowing, asked if she lived there. He said he had just learned that the property was for sale, and would like to look it over, with a view to purchase.

"Would it be convenient?"

Margaret's eyes were full of tears. She was trying to keep stern control over them until far away, but it was hard work. To ask her such a question now! She cast a reproachful look at him and said, almost curtly, that those within would attend to his request.

He watched her as she went swiftly on, admired the pose of her head, the grace of her walk, and the trimness of her brown suit. He said to himself:

"She has beautiful eyes, but they were full of tears. Poor child!"

And then each went their way, little knowing what the years held for them.

The family physician, who came out from the city to attend Mr. Wayland, advised his removal to the hospital, and preparations to that effect were at once made. Old friends warmly offered Mrs. Wayland a temporary home with themselves, and with one of them she was to go for a time. This was the keenest blow of all to the old couple. Somehow they had not counted on separation. Together they could bear anything, together, "till death do us part." Almost the heart of the poor wife rebelled. She shut herself up for a little to face the bitterness of it alone. Sick and old and poor! And now to be separated! To be reunited ... when?

It was the last night in the old house, and everything in readiness for removal. Mrs. Wayland lighted a candle and went about apparently to see if windows were all fastened; really, to give a last look at rooms filled with sacred memories. How they trooped up before her now. The homecoming when she was a bride—little children's pattering feet; merry-makings; girls in bright gowns flitting through this broad hall and up and down the stairs. Why, she could almost see the fair daughter, Ruth, in white on her wedding night, standing on the landing, turning to give a gay word to someone—and there in that room not long after lay dear Ruth; in white again, still hands folded, sleeping her last sleep. Children all gone on before! She and Nathaniel alone. Alone and sick and poor and old!

She stopped at the window and looked into the moon-lighted garden, keenly conscious that it was not her garden anymore. She opened the door and stepped out upon the broad stone. Sweet scents came up like incense in the spring night. Her tears fell like rain as she passed through the walks. Here was the old summerhouse, where children played and lovers whispered vows. The buds and blossoms of that rose vine had graced bridals and burials all through the years. At the foot of the garden ran the brook; she could hear it splash against the stones. The pale green of the willows that fringed it mingled with the mists, seemed to her fancy like wandering forms of those who once ran and laughed and sang about its banks. Sometimes it was hard to believe they should ever meet again.

It was only a momentary doubt, for, as she came back by the beds, where pinks and roses were still brown and dead, where bulbs lay buried in the dark earth—no sign of life—her heart gave a leap, and she was not more sure that these dry things would soon fill the air with sweetness and that her dear ones, sleeping in Jesus, should one day arise in glory and beauty.

And so standing there, casting glances back over the past, peering timidly into the gloomy future, she could yet look up into the face of Christ and say:

"I am thine; I will take the burden thou layest upon me; I will be patient, my dearest Lord."

And because of this there came to her a strange thrill of hope; even for this life, based upon what she knew not, for surely nothing could be more hopeless than the future stretching before her.

She went last to a bed of lilies of the valley. The resurrection had come to them; their waxen bells were perfect against broad leaves. These flowers were brought to her every morning by Nathaniel that wonderful springtime when she was a bride. She gathered some now, went in and barred the door. She gave the lilies to her husband. He understood. He looked at her with longing sorrowful eyes, then clasped her hand, and she knelt by his chair and bowed her head for the evening prayer. At first it was but silent, then the choked voice said:

"Father, for the love that has blessed our lives, for the long years together, we thank thee. Keep our hearts from breaking when we are separated one from another. And, dear Master, do not deny me this, that thou wilt deal gently with her, my darling wife, that thou wilt comfort and protect her. I cannot protect her now. Carry the lamb we both love in my bosom. We know thou lovest us all. We know these trials must be for our good. Thy will be done. Amen."

In the morning Mrs. Wayland accompanied her

husband to the hospital and left him in one of the narrow white beds which seemed to her like a grave. How would Nathaniel, who never liked to have anyone but herself about him when he was sick, endure it to be waited upon by stranger hands? And then to think nobody knew him as Nathaniel Wayland, the noble Christian gentleman. He was simply "No. 20," one of a row in a certain ward, whose needs were to be attended to like any common fellow. She forgot to mourn over her own desolation in pity for him.

Upon thorough examination of Mr. Wayland's case it was found that if cured at all, recovery would be slow, as there were other and more serious complications than rheumatism.

Mrs. Wayland was no common woman. It was not in her energetic nature to sit down content, depending upon the bounty of friends, be they ever so kind, especially when there were no ties of blood between them.

She had suggested to Dr. Morris, their physician, that she was a good nurse and might assist at nursing in the hospital if she could secure a place; but he had laughingly answered that her pretty white hair stood in the way; they could not receive one of her years. When day after day went by—empty, hopeless, monotonous, but with occasional visits to the hospital to vary them—

she betook herself to prayer, pleading:

"The way seems all shut up, dear Lord, but thou canst open it. Please let me go to him. I will do any work thou givest me, however low and mean."

One day a sudden scheme sent her to her room with an eager air. Several years before during severe illness, she was in danger of losing her hair, so it had been cut off and made into a sort of wig to protect her head until a second growth should appear. From a box of relics she produced it now. Mrs. Wayland tried it on. It was the iron-gray hair of a middle-aged person, and the effect was satisfactory. Then a new difficulty presented itself, a moral one.

"It would be a sort of deceit, I suppose," she thought. "Have I a right to make anybody think I am younger than I am? If I feel young, whose concern is it how old I am? They don't care a straw only so I can do the work. It's my old white head that does the deceiving! That says I am not able to work, and I am."

So the matter was settled and perfectly clear to her own conscience, whether you agree with her not.

Discovering that Dr. Morris would come to see a patient in the neighborhood the next day, she left word for him to call upon her. A little before he was expected this intriguing old lady went to her room and changed her black cashmere dress for a neat print one. Then she brushed her white hair carefully away from her face and adjusted the wig, tying over it a cop of the sort worn by nurses. An ample white apron completed the cost.

No, she added an extra, which nurses, as a rule, do not indulge in. It was a creamy white handkerchief in soft folds about her neck and crossed in front. The whole thing was immensely becoming, and she looked twenty years younger. Not every old lady could have so believed Father Time's record, but Mrs. Wayland was remarkably well preserved; her color was still fresh and her eyes retain much of the brightness of youth. The gray hair waved naturally about her for head, and altogether, with her benevolent face and kind eyes, she seemed like a hospital nurse, who would be exceedingly popular among the patients.

When Dr. Morris came into the room where she awaited him, he asked this good-looking, middle-aged woman if she would be so kind as to tell Mrs. Wayland that he was in haste, and had but a few minutes to give her.

"And Mrs. Wayland is in haste, too, doctor," she said, chuckling in triumph at the success of her disguise. "Here she is at your service, sir."

"Upon my word!" And Dr. Morris put on his glasses and stepped nearer. "Well, you're a success, you are, that's a fact. You look about forty-five. Just in your prime! What won't a woman think of?"

"Doctor," said Mrs. Wayland, "I am strong and well. I am a good nurse, you know I am. I want to go into the hospital and help nurse. Won't you use your influence to put me there?"

"My dear madam," Dr. Morris answered, "you can't mean it. All your previous life unfits you for such a place. It would be a different thing entirely from nursing your own in your pleasant home with somebody to wait upon you. Why, you yourself would have to be at beck and call like a servant. You could never stand it. You would be called upon to perform unpleasant duties. You would lose your rest and break yourself down. You don't know how hard and wearisome it is."

"Dr. Morris," and her calm eyes looked straight into his, "I do know, and I do mean it. I can take care of myself. I shall not break down. And it is no fine lady place I am asking for. If you know of any vile work that nobody else is willing to do, give it to me. There is nothing I will not do or bear to be with my husband. It is all I ask in this life. Just try me, doctor. You have always been a good friend to us. Won't you please do this for me?"

"Yes, I will. I'll see to it tomorrow," and Dr. Morris drew his hand across his eyes to dash away a tear, then said: "Good night. God bless you," and was gone.

Mrs. Wayland laid herself down to sleep, with strong hope, for she knew that Dr. Morris's influence in that hospital was without limit.

It was but a few days from that time when, to her great joy, Mrs. Wayland found herself regularly engaged as a nurse in the city hospital with fair compensation. Dr. Morris never did things by halves, and had smoothed the way for her in every direction. He was the more ready to do this because he knew her as a prudent, wise woman, with intuitions about nursing sometimes more valuable than mere technical knowledge.

He had wheedled the board into omitting many of the usual preliminaries in installing nurses, and had ridden over all precedents, and arranged that her labors were to be in the daytime only, as light and agreeable as possible, and that No. 20 was to be her special care. When he had conducted her to her post and heard her grateful thanks he went away with a glow at his heart, for there is no pleasure like giving happiness to others.

Mrs. Wayland had arranged that her husband should not know of her presence in that hospital so that she might surprise him. That morning, after her arrival, he awoke to another wearisome day, feeling unusually depressed. Much of the night had been sleepless, because of pain. The outlook was gloomy. He gazed by the gray light of the morning down the long rows of beds, and sighed, and said to himself, "How long?" What would he not give to have his wife bent over him, and lay her soft hand on his forehead and bathe his head as she used to do? For once his faith seemed weak and his spirit broken. He was hungering for the loving companionship of her who had scarcely left his side during the long life journey, and any probability of her being with him, except an occasional hour, was utterly hopeless. It was hard, so hard. His fellow-patients were all asleep, and the watching nurse was far off, so he did not try to stay the flowing tears.

It was broad daylight and things were astir in the hospital, though the occupant of No. 20 had fallen into a light slumber, from which he awoke to see a nurse stepping briskly about.

He watched her as, with her back to him, she straightened the clothes on the neighboring beds. There was something strangely familiar about her form and walk, and how nice that soft white handkerchief looked, folded about her neck. It was something different and refreshing. The other nurse was tall and large, but this was a little woman. Now she came to his bed and smoothed out the covering. She put back a stray lock of his hair and laid her hand on his forehead. The old man turned and gave her a searching look. She smiled at him. Then he exclaimed, under his breath, "Elizabeth!" and grasped her hand.

"Yes, I've come, Nathaniel. I've come to stay! I had to fix up so as to try to look young," she whispered, "but I didn't think you would know me so quick."

"I'd know the touch of your hand anywhere," murmured the lover of a lifetime. "Tell me all about it."

"I can't now, dear, I must go and get you some breakfast, and you must keep it still who I am, or every poor fellow here will want his wife to come and nurse him."

"Elizabeth, God is good," he whispered, closing his eyes in great content.

Not many weeks passed before nurse Wayland was a privileged character in the hospital. She was allowed to prepare her husband's meals with her own hands, and have entire charge of him. It need not be said that it was better than medicine to him. But she was efficient in other ways; many another sufferer had from her what he longed for above all else—a little mothering. She used to read aloud to her husband in low tones, but so many ears were strained to catch the words that she began to read for the benefit of all in the vicinity, and the hour was eagerly look forward to. Some heard for the first time the words of Scripture from her lips. After a little there was an understanding between the nurse and her patient that much of the reading should be for the benefit of those who needed religious instruction. Sometimes the words of sweet hymns repeated in a low tone would soothe many wakeful ones to sleep. In time she acted almost the part of a chaplain. If any poor fellow required special comforting or had need of a confidant, nobody would answer but Nurse Wayland. Her services were so much petitioned for in this way that finally she was released from all other duties except the care of her husband, and allowed to spend her time as she would among the patients. It was a great delight to her to be of use in this way. So the menial labor that she was willing to do never fell to her lot. God loves to surprise his children and give them the best when they are willing to take the meanest.

Three years past away finding the Waylands still at the hospital, and here they were obliged to stay, as it furnished the only means for earning a livelihood. Mr. Wayland, though still somewhat of an invalid, was able to assist in the dispensary a few hours each day, and his wife's valuable services were gladly retained, for which and her continued strength she gave daily thanks.

The years had brought to Margaret the rich culture she craved, though much as she enjoyed the study, her one eager aim was to enter upon her work and earn a home and needed rest for her grandparents.

She had not been without her romances and her maiden dreams, but they had been resolutely put away. The path was mapped out for her. It was straight and narrow. Some of life's lovely gifts were never to crown her; she had a vocation, a high calling, and it was dear and sweet to anticipate. She did not murmur. It is true that she had not been strongly tempted, for among the young men who had thus far crossed her path, her finely strong nature with its high moral standards had been oftener jarred than attracted.

And now being graduated and fully equipped she faced her lot with all the enthusiasm and confidence of youth. She could not at present hope for a position in the school where she was educated as there was no vacancy, but she was sanguine of securing one somewhere.

Month after month passed in not patient waiting. It would seem that there was some strange fate about it. Every position she applied for had just been filled. She grew hopeless, almost distracted. At last she succeeded in securing a position in the city as visiting governess at remuneration barely sufficient to maintain her in the very cheapest boardinghouse that was respectable. She was thankful even for that, something better would surely come. But the year passed away and it did not come. Life grew to be dreary. She had her seasons of deepest gloom when the forlorn home seemed a prison, when hope for the future died out and even God seemed unreal.

She had her sore temptation, too. A man of wealth and high standing, a good man withal, but many years her senior, asked her to be his wife. If she could but love him how it would smooth the way, for he knew the family and had assured her that her grandparents should be cared for by him. Was it not her duty to accept him for their sakes? She tried to reason with herself. She greatly esteemed him. Might not that stand in the place of that subtle, elusive, mysterious something people called "love"? And yet neither heart nor conscience would entirely acquiesce. While she was thus tossed about in her mind, debating, vacillating, she came upon this bit from the pen of one whose name was often in public print. It was from an article on the subject of divorce and read:

"Not even to save life is a woman justified in promising at the altar to love a man whom she does not love. It is a lie to God and man, a hideous sin, a profanation of the sacred ordinance of marriage as instituted by God. The foundation stone of a true marriage is affection—the truest and tenderest. Mere esteem will not suffice."

This was just the word Margaret needed to save her. It came with all the more force because she had noticed this writer's articles before—that there was a ring about them, a sort of persuasive convincing force. It was signed John Prentiss.

"He must be some wise, grand man," she concluded, "who speaks with so much authority."

She cut out the article and treasured it; there was no more indecision. She began to feel guilty that she had entertained the thought of this marriage for one moment, so disregarding God-given intuitions. And yet it was not for herself she coveted Mr. Oliphant's wealth and beautiful home.

One Saturday Margaret took refuge from her cold room in the parlor, a dingy room dignified by that name. The dreariness within was only exceeded by that without: dark skies and rain, a steady pour. There was just one mitigating circumstance. She was safe from intrusion by the other borders whom business would keep them away until night. If only she had a good story now to make her forget herself. But that was out of the question. Whatever should she do with this day?

She had brought down a pencil and tablet to begin one of the journal-like letters she often wrote her grandmother. But she did not feel quite in the mood yet. Suddenly there flashed into her mind, "Why not write a story myself?" Could she?

She seized the pencil and tablet and began purely for amusement to write out a story suggested by a young lady she had often met on the street in a wheeled chair. Her crippled condition and her sweet face had aroused Margaret's strongest sympathy. She had imagined the story of her life, and had often gone over it again adding to it, until now it was a vivid picture, almost reality, and flowed from her pen easily and naturally. For the first time in many months she had found something aside from a book which absorbed and delighted her. She had run up to the grim stove and shivered at first, but as the pages began to fill up there was no need for artificial heat; her cheeks flushed and her eyes glowed as she went on, surprised that happy turns and phrases should come to her as by magic. Ah, this was a pleasure! Why had she not thought of it before? The eager writer snatched but a few moments for lunch and then went back to her delightful task.

The light was fast-growing dim when she finished it and drew nearer the window to read it over. And now the keen disappointment nearly all writers have experienced came to her. The story was exquisitely told, but she did not know it. It fell so far short of the glowing fancies of her brain, so much of the beauty and fragrance and subtle something which seemed to invest it as she wrote had escaped! It all seemed tame and commonplace. She went up to her room, tossed the tablet into her trunk, told herself she was a foolish creature to imagine she could write, then smoothed her hair and went down to a dimly-lighted dining room to sit at a long table among clerks and drummers and seamstresses and eat a dinner of tough meat, watery potatoes, sour bread and strong butter.

She never lingered in the parlor in the evenings; it was filled by uncongenial company. She went to her fireless room, wrapped herself in an old comfortable and wrote a letter to her grandmother. But in it there was not a hint of chilled fingers or miserable dinner.

Margaret's story had lain in her trunk a month. One day in search for something she came upon it and read it over again. It was not so bad after all. What if she should send it to some newspaper and be paid ever so little for it? The suggestion almost took her breath away. While she made her bed and tidied up her room she thought it over, then came to a sudden resolve. She would try it. It could not harm her to have it returned. She would devote this Saturday to it. So the manuscript was carefully rewritten and sent to one of the prominent religious newspapers.

There followed, of course, the torture of suspense. There were days when she stolidly tried to pretend to herself that she did not "care anything about the matter anyway." At other times she listened for the postman's ring in a nervous tremor with a faint hope fluttering at her heart that at last it had come, a letter for her. And it held a check for five dollars, perhaps! And there were times when she knew positively that she should never hear anything from her story. To this gloomy belief she had settled down when, behold! A letter bearing the stamp of the newspaper office was in her hands. It was not the manuscript returned; the letter was too thin for that. Trembling fingers opened it and found—five dollars? Fifteen dollars! And an invitation to write again. Was Margaret ever so jubilantly happy in her life again? She thanked God and took courage.

The days were dreary no longer. Every moment that could be spared from other duties was given to writing. Not that she spun off stories easily like that first one. That was an inspiration, besides it had simmered in her mind for weeks; each time she had met the girl her fancy wove an added bit. She was long in pleasing herself again, writing and rewriting with exceeding care, sometimes wrestling for hours over a refractory thought or sentence. And now she proved the value of her grandfather's instructions. He was accustomed to give her a theme upon which to write, require her to fill a certain number of pages, then go over it repeatedly, pruning it of every word which did not add strength to a paragraph.

After sending another story to the same paper which was accepted, she began to write articles and sketches for other newspapers.

When, at last, she was requested to become a regular contributor to the paper which accepted her first story, why, then, Margaret took heart of grace, and the home for her grandparents began to seem a sometime possibility. After a few months she ventured upon more ambitious work, and sent a story upon which much labor had been bestowed to a magazine of repute in the literary world. She blushed at her temerity when doing so, for her success was an utter surprise, and unaccountable when she recollected all she had heard and read of the struggles of other writers. However, she was not in the least aware that she possessed talent for this particular work amounting to genius. Neither did she take into account that she had been early taught to read the best authors, to think, and to form a direct and simple style of expression. The result was an excellence, rarely attained except by long years of practice, and sometimes not then.

Margaret had reasons for choosing the particular magazine she did. It was not of the higher sort. Moreover, its editor was John Prentiss, and name which had become to her a sort of talisman. She had decided, too, that he was an elderly man of kindly judgment; perhaps he would so judge her story.

Mr. John Prentiss sat in his office reading manuscripts. He was not so very venerable, having just passed thirty. As to looks, he had a plain, smooth, strong face, lighted—positively lighted—by eyes which reminded one of lamps or stars. As he bent his head over his work his fingers occasionally tossed his abundant dark hair into becoming disorder. He was unmarried, for the same reason that many women have for walking through life alone: he never yet had found the one with whom he wished to walk.

Since early manhood, his aged mother, a woman of beautiful character, had been his precious charge. Perhaps this was the reason her son had added to his sterner virtues that rare courtesy of manner which distinguished him among men. Not that he was effusive; he was considerately kind. His manner toward womankind had just that blending of chivalry and reverence which always charms a woman. His "Good morning" was like a benediction; one felt that he had in those two words expressed all sorts of good wishes.

When he exchanged a few sentences—even with his washerwoman—she felt his kindly interest and went on with the comfortable feeling of self-respect. One of his elderly lady friends remarked that "It was a pity John Prentiss did not marry, just to show one woman how royally she can be cared for." This friend knew that he did not put on his best manners with his best coat, and that the members of his own household were not treated to indifference, glum silence, or irritating words, while he dispensed sunshine and sweetness to the outside world. After all, it was more the things he did not do that made John Prentiss so agreeable. Unlike many men of literary pursuits, he did not forget all the small courtesies of life because he was absorbed in his own thoughts.

He opened Margaret's manuscript wearily. It was one of a large pile he had read that day, or partly read; he needed but a few pages of some to consign them to the wastebasket or return them to their owners. Over this one he lingered, reading it through to the end, then exclaimed:

"This is positively refreshing."

"A beautiful story," he remarked to a man at another desk, "by the author of 'Dorothea's Outings'—an exquisite little thing published in one of our exchanges. I'm glad of this manuscript. The woman, whoever she is, has true genius and does not write merely to amuse. Her style is simple yet vigorous. There is much thought in her work and the outgoings of a pure, healthy nature. It often hurts my conscience to publish such trash in the form of stories as we sometimes do. Young people should be elevated by Christian editors, not pulled downward."

Margaret's story had lain many weeks in the office before Mr. Prentiss had found leisure to examine it. Meanwhile its author had been passing through the chills and fevers of suspense, after suffering tortures of mortification that she should have been so presuming as to send anything to that magazine of all others. But she was again amazed and overjoyed at its acceptance and a check that to her seemed perfectly munificent. Nor was this all. It was accompanied by a note expressing the editor's kind appreciation of her work.

"It is just like that good, noble man," Margaret told herself in a perfect transport of delight. She wished so much for somebody to run and tell it to, but there was nobody. So she sat down and wrote it to the two old people who treasured every word of hers as if it were gold dust.

Into the boarding house where Margaret lived there had lately come a sad young widow with her child. The little fellow was lonely and restless, especially in bad weather when he could not get out. Margaret often took pity on him when her work was done, and whiled away a half hour of his time in a romp or childish game.

One dreary day when rain was dripping from gray skies, Margaret challenged him to catch her. She taught him to run on tiptoe so as to make no noise. They ran the length of the long hall into the back door of the parlor, through that room and into the hall by the other door, and so back down the hall again. The fun had been going on some time accompanied by little squeals and bursts of subdued laughter, when almost the victim would be within the boy's grasp and then escape again. Scurrying in high glee up the hall they came face to face with a tall man whom Bridget had just admitted! Divested of dripping Macintosh and hat he was distinguished-looking, Margaret thought, as she sought to escape through the back hall. But Bridget intercepted her and handed her a card. To her dismay the name on it was "John Prentiss."

There was no time to retreat to her room and brush her hair which during the race had escaped in disorderly rings and waves about her face. To meet the great editor in this way! How aggravating!

Now, Mr. Prentiss always had a well-defined idea as to the personal appearance of people he had heard of and never met. He was sure, for instance, that Miss Margaret Wayland was a woman of mature years, with sharp, thin, dark face, hooked nose, tired eyes, drooping corners to her mouth, and scanty hair, done in a small hard knot; also, she lived in a cheap boardinghouse.

"'Here it is, just as I thought,'" he said to himself, as he pulled the reluctant bell handle.

When Margaret advanced toward him with a lovely flush the exercise had called up, deepening and glowing, she did not in the least look her twenty-four years. He was incredulous. This slim, straight girl, with innocent eyes—where had he seen those eyes before?—with rounded cheeks and infantile curves of her mouth, was charming, but not in the least like what he had fancied his new contributor to be.

Mr. Prentiss was a self-possessed man on all occasions, but he felt half embarrassed now when he recollected the errand upon which he had come. It seemed so preposterous to talk to this pretty, laughing girl about furnishing a serial for their magazine. There must be some mistake. There were probably two Miss Waylands.

But Margaret was also taken aback by his appearance. If she had spoken out her thoughts, they would have been: "And you are the editor! I thought he would be an oldish man, stout, with a massive head, rather bald, fringed with gray hair, and very kind eyes."

Mr. Prentiss, however, was quite reassured after a

few moment's conversation. The same thoughtfulness, simplicity and directness which characterized her writing was in her words and manner, and charmed him a new.

There was discernible, too, a certain maturity—a sort of patient sweetness—not usually found in the character of a young woman, unless she has suffered and grown strong thereby. When Mr. Prentiss made known the object of his call Margaret was overwhelmed. Dare she undertakes so great a thing? She frankly told him her misgivings, and asked for time to consider, although he assured her they would have no fears of the result if she consented.

"But I am so very grateful to you for the invitation," she told him, with shining eyes. "You cannot know what it is to me to be so encouraged."

Mr. Prentiss was not accounted an absent-minded man, but that day must be an exception. He walked off in a pouring rain, and left his umbrella in the hall of the boardinghouse, and never discovered the omission till he had tramped the length of several squares, then he looked up in surprise at the dull sky, and said, within himself, "I thought the sun was shining!"

After much trepidation and counselings with herself, Margaret decided to attempt the serial. She ceased to wish for a position in the school, as the present arrangement left her much leisure. The days flew rapidly by. There was no time now to gloom, if she had felt like it. Her work was delightful and all-absorbing.

Life, too, was brightened for her in another, most un-looked for a way. Mr. Prentiss, since that memorable day, had often called, had occasionally taken her to a lecture or concert. And he dropped in for a half-hour's chat at that dreariest time of the day to a lonely person: the early winter twilight.

Margaret, mindful of her resolution made months ago, had to take herself seriously to task at times, lest she should delight too much in the society of this genial, cultured friend. She must not allow anyone to divert her from her one purpose. She told herself that she was as much set aside, devoted, as any man. At last she was nearing the goal! By the strictest economy, continuing in a cheap boardinghouse, and other self-denials, she might feel justified in making a home for her grandparents by another year. And that should be happiness enough for her. She must not covet for herself that other blessed lot which falls to some. This thought—that she must keep her heart well in hand—had the effect of imparting to her manner toward Mister Prentiss a reserve and indifference she did not at all feel.

One morning in early spring, Margaret threw up

her window and, kneeling down by it, leaned her head far out in the effort to get a whiff of air that was not laden with fried pork or some other undesirable scent. It was utterly useless to try, though. Next door was the restaurant, the odor of fried onions was there. There was a bakery on the other side, and fried cakes and burnt bread steamed up from there, and fumes, vile, indescribable, came up from the street gutter. She lifted her eyes to the bit of blue sky, visible between roofs, and sighed, and thought what it would be to be in a place for a little where there were no odors of any description; just pure, sweet, fresh clean air.

As if in response to this longing came a messenger with a bunch of violence and a note. It read:

"Dear Ms. Wayland, don't you want a breath of fresh air? I have promised to take my aunt out in the country this afternoon, and we covet the pleasure of your company.

"While Aunt Elsie makes her visit you and I can drive on farther to a lovely waterfall I know of. There is also a fine view to be enjoyed from that hilltop.

Your friend,

JOHN PRENTISS."

Margaret did not wait to take counsel of any inward advisors or tormenting suggestions of prudence. To the country she was going. And she wrote a note of acceptance in a perfect flutter of delight; then trod on air all the morning. She read the note over occasionally, and liked the looks of the words, "You and I."

Punctually at one o'clock the carriage drove up, and Margaret was placed in the backseat with Aunt Elsie, a pleasant old lady who called her "dear," and told her how much she liked her stories.

"How long do you wish to stay, auntie?" Mr. Prentiss asked as he left her at the door.

"Oh, an hour or two," she answered.

"That means three hours at least by Aunt Elsie's reckoning," her nephew remarked with satisfaction, as he gathered up the reins and looked back at Margaret with a smile which seemed somehow to bring to her mind the words in his note, "You and I." She flushed at that, and was sorry she had thought of it.

The air was divine, not as Margaret had wished it, odorless, but filled with all spring fragrances of wood and grass and fruit blossoms. They were silent for a time, content not to speak, just to be exulting in it all, for it seems they had not realized the sweetness until left by themselves.

"I fancy we are somewhat alike," Mr. Prentiss said

at last. "When we go to see Mother Nature we want her to do the talking while we keep silence. Isn't that so?"

And Margaret nodded smiling assent.

Truth to tell, though, Mr. Prentiss was not entirely occupied with nature's charms that day. He was trying to solve a problem which had to do with Margaret herself. She was intent only on losing nothing of the glory and beauty about her. It was a perfectly perplexing study, and he had gone over it more than once. Why, he asked himself, did this girl who seemed to enjoy his society, maintain a certain reserve toward him, baffling all attempts to speak words that meant more than mere friendship, unless what he feared was true, that she was pledged to another? From the first day he met her that had been to him an unwelcome suggestion. It was fast becoming an unbearable one. For his own peace of mind he must know the truth. There was just one small thing that gave him slight comfort. He had seen her face once when she met him unexpectedly, light up in that indescribably joyful way! A look that one person only has the power to call forth from another. It was but a flash though, the next instant it was gone. She was a puzzle, but she was not a flirt, of that he was sure. She was too undeniably sweet and true for that. She was transparent. As well charge a mountain stream with acting a part.

Now they came upon a delightful bit of woods where the undergrowth was cleared and tree trunks were outlined against the sky, and green vistas stretched far out in front and on either side. There were clumps of wood violets and patches of bright moss and maiden hair ferns. Margaret exclaimed with delight, and the carriage stopped while they looked.

"I wonder if those people in that house live up to their privileges?" she said, pointing to a pretentious farmhouse not far off. "All this beauty and sweetness so near them."

"Not they," Mr. Prentiss answered. "They would doubtless exchange it all for a set of lace curtains or a fine chair. But perhaps I do them an injustice; here is a seat under an old beech tree where somebody probably sits to worship at Nature's shrine."

He stepped out as he spoke and held out his hand.

"Have we got there?" Margaret asked.

"No, not for where we started, but I know by your looks that you want some of these violets and ferns."

They made little excursions from one side to another, busily talking and gathering all sorts of treasures.

"Oh, if I could take a little root of these ferns," Margaret said, bending over them, "but I can't."

"But you can. Aunt Elsie forages about here and

carries a trowel in the carriage." In another moment the fern was dug up placed in the carriage.

"Now command me further," he said, regarding her again with a look few people beside his mother had ever seen.

They drifted after a time to the seat under the tree and half-unconsciously sat down, going on with talk of which they never tired. It was so delightful to each to know that their views, peculiar sometimes, harmonized on so many different subjects. But then they did not harmonize. Mr. Prentiss enjoyed it almost more than when they did. It was so for refreshing to hear a woman argue logically, not raise her voice above ordinary tones, not grow red in the face, nor rant, nor snap her eyes and say ugly things. He abhorred sarcasm in a woman.

But this girl, with a certain sweet gravity, stated her points in a clear-cut way, yet in low, persuasive tones, a wistful look meanwhile in her eyes, as if she were sure he was wrong, and she did so long that he should find the truth, but yet recognizing the right of each to judge for himself. As the talk went on Mr. Prentiss told her of his happy boyhood home and all about a dear sister who had died in her youth, and that with the death of his father not long after, had cast a cloud over his early manhood; how he and his old mother had lived together alone after that, devoted to each other.

"Two years ago," he said, with husky voice, "she went to the other side and left me here, how lonely God only knows."

Margaret's eager, sympathetic listening was precious to him just now when he was picking up every straw that could possibly tell anything on the question as to where he stood in her regard. She asked more about his sister.

"I do want to tell you a sweet little thing about her," he said. "As a child she was peculiarly lovely, the most affectionate little creature that can be imagined. She used to be much alone with mother. Sometimes as they sat together, mother sewing and Edith, not much more than a baby, with her bit of sewing, her little chair drawn close by mother's, inexpressibly happy, would rock back and forth in joyful content, and then look up and mother's face, with loving eyes, and murmur: 'You and I! You and I!'"

Mr. Prentiss wondered then at the rosy glow that spread Margaret's face. She was going back to those words in the letter, but how should he know it?

"That has been a dear and much-quoted phrase in our family ever since," he went on, "said when we wished to express much in fewest words. Should I be presuming if I say it now to you, meaning to convey all that she did—unspeakable, tenderest devotion. Dare I hope that we may be thus together through life and forever more—'You and I?'"

Again he saw that flash in Margaret's face for an instant, a look of unutterable joy, but it was gone and a shadow took its place as she murmured:

"No, I—I—you must not say such things to me."

"Oh! It is as I feared, then. There is somebody else," he said gloomily.

"No! There is not!" emphatically.

"You are indifferent to me, then?"

Margaret's protest was in her eyes as she lifted them to his. He did not need the low-spoken, "No."

"Will you tell me what is in the way, then?"

"I have taken a vow," she murmured.

"Vow? Are you a nun?" And merry gleam came into his eyes. "Can't you tell me about it?"

Margaret had never spoken much about herself to him. She told him now of her old home, painted the portraits of her grandparents with loving touches, told of their losses in poverty, her own struggles and discouragements. But thanks to him, the clouds were breaking, and she had saved nearly enough to allow her to begin a new home.

"Then," she said, "I expect to devote myself to my grandparents and try to make the rest of their lives comfortable and happy."

"I must say, I see no obstacles yet," Mr. Prentiss answered, joyfully. "Don't you think two can take care of your grandparents better than one? Let me help you perform your vow. I do not remember either grandfather or grandmother of my own. I should feel myself grown immensely rich to come into such a possession."

Margaret was silent a moment, though she could not keep the gladness from her eyes. One thing she had kept back.

"I must tell him all," she said to herself, then aloud: "Perhaps you will repent your words when I tell you something more."

"Tell on, my dear contributor."

"My grandmother is a hospital nurse!"

"It makes no difference to me if she is a washerwoman."

Margaret broke into a laugh then.

"Is it 'You and I' forever?" He put out his hand. For answer Margaret laid hers in his.

And then Mr. Prentiss must needs hear every smallest detail of Margaret's life; everything was of intensest interest that concerned her or hers.

"All honor to your grandmother," he said, when told of her little piece of strategy and her years of self-denial. "She is a heroine and I shall rejoice to have her for mine.

There is just one thing, though, in your past history that arouses my jealousy."

Margaret had told him of her temptation to marry Mr. Oliphant and that his own words were the means of saving her.

"I do not understand," he said, "why you were willing this man should care for your grandparents, but did not intend to give me that privilege, actually putting them up as a hindrance in my way."

"He—he proposed for them," she said, demurely. "You asked only for myself. I couldn't accept for all three of us." And then the birds and squirrels were startled by a merry laugh from both of them. Often, as when he first met her, there had flitted before Mr. Prentiss a tantalizing memory of having seen her before.

"Somewhere, Margaret," he told her now, "your eyes have looked into mine before. There is only one pair on the earth of this description. I am sure of it. Perhaps it was in a pre-historic age we met."

With all this talk they forgot the view and the waterfall and were only warned by lengthening shadows that it was more than time to go for Aunt Elsie.

A few days afterward Mr. Prentiss took Margaret for a long drive ten miles into the country to show her the summer home he had purchased for his mother a few years before. It had been leased since her death, he told her, adding, with one of those rare smiles, which meant a blessing or a caress:

"It shall be vacated soon. We will fit it up in a charming way and flit to it whenever we tire of the city. I hope you will like the quaint old place."

As they drove through the gateway Margaret cast an astonished look at him, exclaiming in delight:

"Why, this is my old home! My grandfather's place!"

Then a sudden revelation came to John Prentiss.

"And it was here I saw you when I came to look at it, just there by the gate, and you had tears in your pretty eyes."

"Yes, and you were on horseback," Margaret said slowly, trying to recall. "I must've looked cross at you. I recollect somebody asking me about the place, and I felt so sore-hearted. To think it was you!"

"To think it was you!" Mr. Prentiss exclaimed, bringing his horse to a full stop while he gazed at the spot where they both stood that day. "Passed you by and did not know my other self! How cruel in me to buy the roof from over your head! If I had but known! I watched you, though, after you passed, dear. I sympathized in your grief and I never forgot your eyes. That was more than you did for me. You marched straight on and never gave me a second thought."

It was Christmas Eve when Margaret Prentiss and her husband welcomed their grandparents to the old homestead. Rooms devoted to them had been made bright and beautiful with all that ingenuity and love could suggest. The fire on the white hearth, and their easy chairs standing side by side seemed just as they had left them five years ago.

Together they sit, these two, through the golden days of life's sunset. An ideal marriage it was; love undimmed through a half century! God be thanked that hearts do not grow old.

> "O, lay thine hand in mine, dear,
>   We're growing old;
> But time hath wrought no sign, dear,
>   That hearts grow cold.
> 'Tis long, long since our new love
>   Made life divine;
> But age enricheth true love,
>   Dear, lay thine hand in mine."

Books by
Marcia Livingston

(writing as Mrs. C. M. Livingston)

Aunt Hannah and Martha and John *

By Way of the Wilderness *

Divers Women *

From Different Standpoints *

John Remington, Martyr *

Kathy Hunter's Homes

The Night Before Christmas; A Christmas Exercise

Profiles *

The Kaleidoscope (co-written with her sister Isabella Alden)

A Sevenfold Trouble **

The Story of Puff

Susan's Sheaves and Other Stories

* Co-written with her sister Isabella Alden

** Co-written with Isabella Alden, Grace Livingston Hill and others

Books by
Grace Livingston Hill

According to the Pattern
All Through the Night
Amorelle
The Angel of His Presence
April Gold
Ariel Custer
Astra
Aunt Crete's Emancipation
Beauty for Ashes
Because of Stephen
Beggerman
The Beloved Stranger
The Best Birthday
The Best Man
The Big Blue Soldier
Blue Ruin
Brentwood
Bright Arrows
By Way of the Silverthorns
The Challengers
The Chance of a Lifetime
A Chautauqua Idyl
The Christmas Bride
The City of Fire
Cloudy Jewel
A Colonial Girl
Coming Through the Rye
Crimson Mountain
Crimson Roses
A Daily Rate
Daphne Deane
Dawn of the Morning

A Divided Battle
Duskin
Dwelling
The Enchanted Barn
The Esselstynes, or,
    Alphonso and
    Marguerite
Exit Betty
The Finding of Jasper Holt
The Forgotten Friend
Found Treasure
The Girl from Montana
The Girl of the Woods
A Girl to Come Home to
The Gold Shoe
Happiness Hill
Head of the House
Her Wedding Garment
Homing
The Honeymoon House
The Honor Girl
The House Across the
Hedge
In the Way
In Tune with Wedding
Bells
Job's Niece
Katherine's Yesterday and
    Other Christian
    Endeavor Stories
Kerry
Ladybird

Lo, Michael
Lone Point
The Lost Message
The Man of the Desert
Marcia Schuyler
Marigold
Maris
Mary Arden *
Matched Pearls
Memories of Yesterdays
The Minister's Son
Miranda
Miss Lavinia's Call, and
    Other Stories
More than Conqueror
Mystery Flowers
The Mystery of Mary
A New Name
Not Under the Law
The Obsession of Victoria
    Gracen
Out of the Storm
The Parkerstown Delegate
Partners
The Patch of Blue
Patricia
Phoebe Deane
The Prodigal Girl
Rainbow Cottage
The Ransom
Re-creations

The Red Signal
Rose Galbraith
The Search
The Seventh Hour
The Short Stories of Grace
    Livingston Hill
Silver Wings
The Sound of the Trumpet
Spice Box
The Story of a Whim
The Story of the Lost Star
The Strange Proposal
Stranger Within the Gates
The Street of the City
The Substitute Guest
Sunrise
Through These Fires
Time of the Singing of
    Birds
Tomorrow Abut This Time
The Tryst
An Unwilling Guest
A Voice in the Wilderness
The War Romance of the
    Salvation Army
Where Two Ways Met
The White Flower
The White Lady
White Orchids
The Witness

* Co-written with her daughter Ruth Livingston Hill

Books by
Isabella Alden

(writing as Pansy, or Mrs. G. R. Alden)

After Play Stories
Agatha's Unknown Way: A
    Story of Missionary
    Guidance
An April Walk
An Endless Chain; Workers
    Together
An Hour with Miss Streator
An Interrupted Night
As in a Mirror
At Home and Abroad
At Home Stories
Aunt Hannah and Martha
    and John *
Bernie's White Chicken
Bobby's Wolf and Other
    Stories
The Browning Boys; or,
    Striving to Help
The Browns at Mount Hermon
By Way of the Wilderness *
Callie's Experiment and Other
    Stories
The Chautauqua Girls at Home
Chrissy's Endeavor
Christie's Christmas
A Christmas Time

Couldn't Be Bought
The Cube
Cunning Workmen
Daisy and Grandpa
Danger Cliff and Other Stories
David Ransom's Watch
A Day at Grandpa Bogart's and
    Other Stories
Divers Women *
Docia's Journal, or, God is
    Love
Doris Farrand's Vocation
A Dozen of Them
Dr. Deane's Way and Other
    Stories **
Echoing and Re-echoing *
Eighty-Seven
Emma's Ambition
An Endless Chain
Enlisted
Ester Ried: Asleep and Awake
Ester Ried: Yet Speaking
Ester Ried's Awakening
Ester Ried's Namesake
Eugene Cooper
The Exact Truth
Five Friends

Following Heavenward
The Fortunate Calamity
Four Girls at Chautauqua
Four Mothers at Chautauqua
Frank Hudson's Hedge Fence
    and Other Stories
Fred's House
Fred's Puzzle and Other Stories
From Different Standpoints *
Gertrude's Diary
Getting Ahead
Glimpses of Boyhood
Glimpses of Girlhood
Going Halves
A Golden Thought and Other
    Stories
Grace Holbrook and Other
    Stories of Endeavor
Grandpa's Darlings
The Hall in the Grove
A Happy Summer and Other
    Stories
A Hedge Fence
Helen Lester
Helen the Historian
Her Associate Members
Her Mother's Bible
Her Own Way
Household Puzzles
How He Escaped and Other
    Stories
In the Woods and Out, and
    Other Stories
Interrupted
Jessie Wells; or, How to Save
    the Lost
John Remington, Martyr *

Judge Burnham's Daughters
Julia Ried: Listening and Led
The Kaleidoscope *
The King's Daughter
Laura's Promise
Leafy Fern
Leonard's April Fool
The Lesson in Story
Links in Rebecca's Life
Little by Little
The Little Card
Little Fishers and Their Nets
Little Hands
Little Minnie and Other Stories
A Little Missionary
Little Pansy Library
Little People in Picture and
    Story
The Long Way Home
Lost Nellie
Lost on the Trail
Mag and Margaret; A Story for
    Girls
Making Fate
The Man of the House
Mara
Mary Burton Abroad and Other
    Stories
Memories of Yesterdays
Miss Dee Dunmore Bryant
Miss Doctor Bellby and Other
    Stories
Miss Priscilla Hunter
Missent; or, The Story of a
    Letter
The Mission of a Gray Sock
    and Other Stories

Foreign Lands, First
Series
Young Folks Stories of
Foreign Lands, second
series

Young Folks Story Book
Young Folks Worth
Knowing
Young People Abroad
Young People At Home

* Co-written with her sister Marcia Livingston
** Co-written with Faye Huntington

You can learn more about Isabella Alden, read free novels and stories, and view a complete list of her published books at:

www.IsabellaAlden.com

Made in the USA
Columbia, SC
13 December 2022

73643452R00133